# BECAUSE OF THE HORSES

*by*

Patricia McGrane

McGrane, Patricia
Because Of The Horses: a novel/Patricia McGrane
ISBN: 978-0-9991094-0-3 (paperback) First edition
ISBN: 978-0-9991094-1-0 (ebook)

Credits
Map, Online Format Image, Library of Congress Geography and Map Division, Washington, D.C.

Interior design and Cover design by Ryan Salinetti

Printed by IngramSpark, Nashville, Tennessee

becauseofthehorses.com

Because Of The Horses is fiction. All the characters and situations experienced by the Marsh family and their acquaintances are imaginary.

The setting for the story is rural East Tennessee in the summer of 1863, an area well-known for the strong independent thinking and self-reliance of its citizens. In addition, some were active in the abolitionist movement and a few with the Underground Railroad. They fiercely supported the Union. Others were staunch supporters of the Confederacy and strongly agreed with the formation of a new country. This split in allegiance among the residents resulted in divided families and pitted neighbors against each other, inevitably introducing uneasy and often explosive situations into daily living.

Two small pieces of family history, handed down to me by my mother many years ago, have been nagging me to create this story. One was about a house which had once belonged to her first cousin's family in the early 1900's. It was a big two story house surrounded by farmland and woods, located off the old country road to Jonesborough, Tennessee. Unforgettable to me was that she said the house had once been part of the Underground Railroad and that as young girls, she and her cousin used to spend hours playing in the two tunnels which still existed. One led from the cellar into the woods and creek at the back of the house and the other to a small shallow cave. I can remember wishing that I could play in those tunnels, and although the terms "Cool" and "Who knew?" weren't trendy then, they certainly applied to my impression then and now.

Years went by and then unexpectedly the second little family tidbit, and certainly the most significant, was revealed the day she dug into her desk and pulled out a tattered little black book which she said was a diary kept by my great-great grandfather during the Civil War. The faintly penciled pages documented his activities and ledger entries, not as a soldier, but as a horse trader to both the Union and Confederate armies. Here, in his faded handwriting, was my relative describing his efforts to eke out a living to support his family by slipping back and forth between enemy camps. Sadly, the diary has disappeared, but my imagination has kept the intrigue of his dangerous dealings and the mystery of how he managed it alive and well.

Because Of The Horses is not meant to be historical by any means. It is a story, very loosely based on family lore, about a microcosm of society and events separate from, but being played out within, a much bigger social upheaval.

Patricia McGare

Melbourne Beach, Florida, 2017

"Look back at our struggle for freedom,
Trace our present day's strength to its source;
And you'll find that man's pathway to glory
Is strewn with the bones of the horse."

~ Author Unknown

Mountain Region of North Carolina and Tennessee, 1864,
Online Format Image, Library of Congress Geography and
Map Division, Washington, D.C. (also detailed on next page)

Bristol
Kingsport
Reedy Cr
New Canton
Edgar Ridge
Edgeworth
Blountsville
Lyons
Clover Bottom
Gott's Crossing
Middletown
Union
Taylorsville
Yellow St
Fall's Branch
Shells Sta
Clear Cr
Cherry Grove
Buffalo Ridge
Carters Depot
Laurel Gap
Newmansville
Johnsons
Elizabethtown
Mt Hope
Locust Mt
Jonesboro
Parlewison Wks
Washington College
Tellfords
Rheatown Pullens
Leesburg
Cox's Store
Henderson
Limestone
Cherokee Cr
Buckstone Mt
Greenville
Horse Cr
Tanguira
Gourleys Br
Ceders Br
Cedar Creek
Roan High Knob
Caney Br
Bakersville
Bald Spot
Burnsville
Walnut Mts
Walnut Cr
Cocks Comb
Marshall
Pines Pond
Black Knob
Mt Mitchell
Laurel Mt
Big Creek
Michelangelo
Laurel Cr
Pleasant Garden
Marion
Asheville
Sulphur Sprs
Bald Mountains
Waynesville
Fairview
Hickory Nut Gap
Hendersonville
Court House
Broad River
Columbus
Ruth

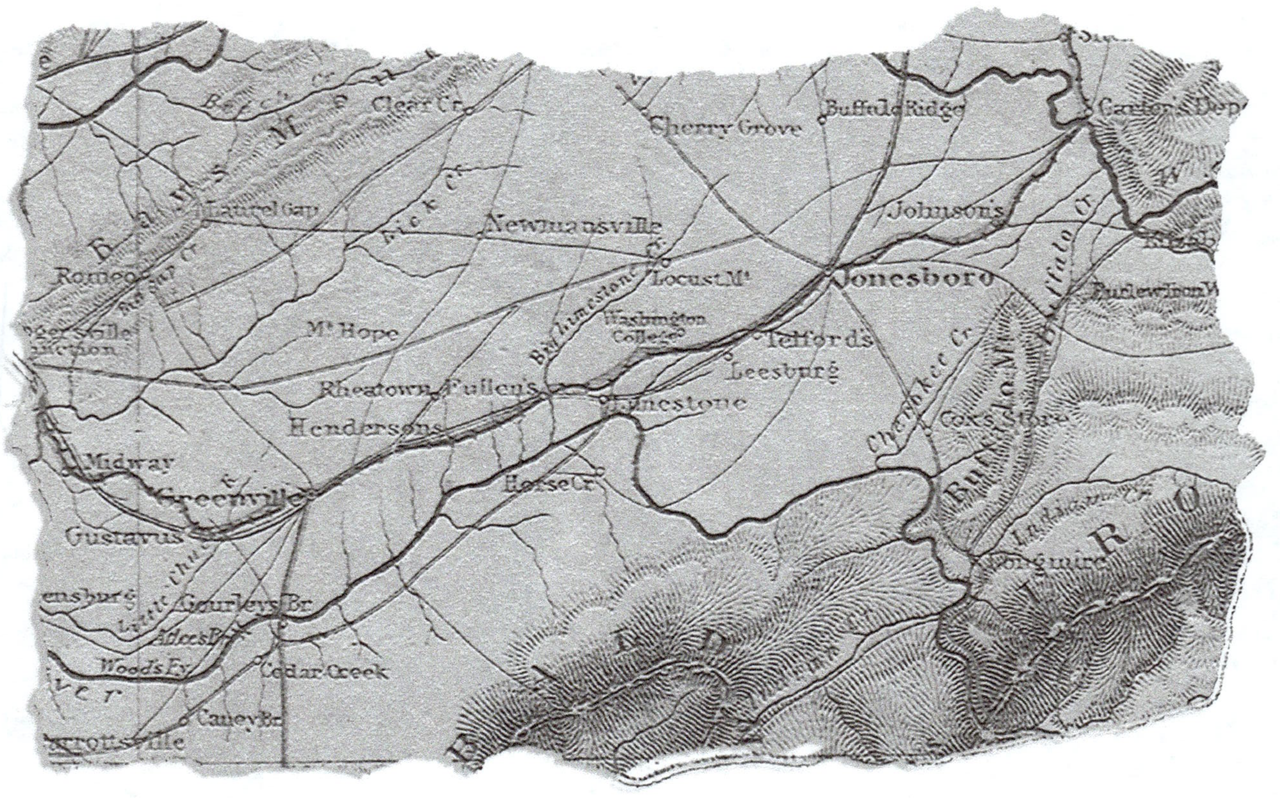
Clear Cr
Cherry Grove
Buffalo Ridge
Carter's Dep
Laurel Gap
Newmansville
Johnson's
Romeo
Locust M
Jonesboro
Purlew Iron W
M Hope
Washington College
Telfords
Leesburg
Rogersville junction
Rheatown
Pullens
Limestone
Cherokee Cr
Cox's Store
Hendersons
Buffalo M
Midway
Horse Cr
Greeneville
Gustavus
ensburg
Gourleys Br
Atkes Fy
Woods Fy
Cedar Creek
Caney Br
rrottsville

*1*

*Diary Entry—June 1, 1863*
*Headed to Afton this morning to officiate at G. Pickering's*
*funeral. Harri won't go. I'll have to make excuses for her.*
*Taking Gray instead of the buggy. That way I can cut*
*through the fields and follow the creek path. Need to stay*
*away from the road—too many soldiers seen marching lately.*
*—E. Marsh*

  Eli wedged his diary into his pocket and headed for the barn just as the sun's rays reached over the hills. Up since first light as usual, saying his morning prayers and making his diary entry, he had slipped out of the house without waking his wife Harriet. Carrying the biscuits and fruit she had packed for him the night before, he thought about the ride to Afton and hoped there would be no delays. The worst problems came when he was stopped by random groups of soldiers who always questioned him. Worse were the roaming bummers who confiscated anything they remotely thought their armies could use. His mission as a Presbyterian minister gave him some protection from this sort of "honorable thievery." So far he had been able to get away safely, but it always cost him valuable time if nothing else.

Reaching the barn, Eli found that his farmhands, Morgan and Ford, had already saddled Gray and had turned the rest of the horses out into the pastures for the day. Freed slaves, they had come to him through the Roberts family in Greeneville who were still active in the Manumission Society of Tennessee. Basically this group believed in the principle of gradual emancipation. They considered it the humane way to assimilate former slaves into the larger community by taking the time to educate and prepare them for life in a free society. Eli thought this an honorable approach, but he never joined the group. Two chapters of the Society still existed nearby in Greeneville and at Washington College farther to the East. Although they were less active since the War started, they still helped former slaves who filtered into the area through the Underground Railroad hoping to find work in the community or help in getting on North. Hiring Morgan and Ford had been a real issue for Harri, but even she admitted now that they were the best workers they had ever had. There seemed to be no job they couldn't or wouldn't take on.

"Thanks. I'll be back before dinner," Eli said taking the reins. "Keep an eye on the house and store and Mrs. Marsh today," he called, as he trotted off across the fields.

The day dragged by for Harriet Marsh. By mid-afternoon, she decided to close up the Bee, her little general store across the road from their house. Only two people had stopped in—just to say hello, not to buy anything—and now she was lonely and anxious for Eli to get home. She wiped down the wooden counter, covered the pies in the glass case, put the lids on the big candy jars and straightened the loose clothes and shoes. The dwindling supply of merchandise and customers made closing up easy these days with hardly any money to count. Before the War started in 1861, the Bee was filled with customers and conversation. Its shelves were stocked to the ceiling with dry goods and sundries. Barrels overflowed with fruits and vegetables. She and Eli and their son Rice would regularly buy supplies in Greeneville, and twice a year in Knoxville to stock their Limestone store. Traveling around East Tennessee, even after the War started, was still fairly easy. Of course that had all changed after the state voted to secede and join the Confederacy, except for East Tennessee which remained fiercely loyal to the Union. Now it wasn't unusual to see or be stopped by troops from either army on the back roads.

While the battles had dragged on in other parts of the country for the last two years, their life as a family had stayed pretty much the same. "Thank the Lord," Harriet said out loud. She was happy running the store which had originally belonged to her father, George Burkhart. Eli was consumed with his pastoral duties for the small Presbyterian congregations dotting the country roads in Greene and Washington Counties. Rice, now twenty, ran the farm and took care of Eli's horses. Harriet knew they were an especially lucky family. Eli was too old to be drafted into Confederate service. That had happened to so many men and boys around them. Plus, he was a man of the cloth, strongly opposed to all war and obsessive in his anti-slavery views and support for Mr. Lincoln. And Rice—well he had been born with a withered right arm and a little stub of a hand which kept him from being fit for soldier material.

Harriet sighed. She still felt the sting of guilt and failure that she had delivered a deformed baby. Eli said it was God's way, but she didn't believe it. It was her fault and she steadfastly refused to ever have another baby. Thankfully, Rice had gotten along just fine and the pathetic arm and hand hadn't kept him from most activities. He was keenly smart and very handsome just like Eli, and he had already earned an embarrassing reputation as a ladies' man. Harriet tried not to listen to the gossip swirling around her about what Rice was up to or who he was seeing, but it still made her heart painful. Eli chose to ignore all that talk, because he vowed Rice was such a good son in every other way.

"Who you talking to this time, Mother?" Rice's voice drifted into Harriet's thoughts.

Harriet jumped, her face turning red. "Just these old stacks of clothes and shoes," she laughed softly. "They never talk back to me like you do! Are you finished for the day already?"

"Not really. Is Pop back yet?" he asked.

"I haven't seen him," she answered. "He should be here by dinner. The funeral in Afton was at noon, and I'm sure he went back to the Pickerings' house after the cemetery. Anything wrong?"

"Nah—Mack Johnson came by the barn earlier and wanted to know if Pop would be interested in taking his horses. He can't keep them up now that Harold and Jimmy both got killed at Vicksburg," he said, looking out the door for his father.

"I declare. Two miserable years of this War and all we have to show for it are more good sons like Harold and Jimmy dying and families barely hanging on. Thank God you and your father aren't part of it," Harriet said angrily.

Rice frowned and kicked open the screen door. He hated it when his mother talked this way. "I would give anything to be there—to be doing something—anything to help," he snapped, walking away from her toward the barn.

Harriet bit her lip hard to make the tightness in her chest go away. She knew Rice felt guilty that his arm had kept him out of the War. So many of his friends had joined the fight on both sides. Now they either weren't coming back or they had been so horribly maimed, their lives were ruined. She meant what she said. She couldn't be more thankful that Eli and Rice couldn't be taken.

Harriet hung the "closed" sign on the door to the Bee. As

she crossed the road to the house, she saw Eli riding down the hill. He looked very tall in the saddle with his wide brimmed hat and his long silvery beard. Even at fifty-three, he was still handsome—well, definitely distinguished. Instead of going to the house, she walked toward the barn so she could meet him.

Eli smiled to himself when he saw Harriet walking towards him. Her long blonde hair, now flecked with strands of white, was held back by tortoise shell combs that glistened in the sun. Even from a distance, he could see her high cheek bones were blushed red from the summer heat. After all their years together, he still felt like the luckiest man alive that she was his wife. When she smiled and kissed him or held his hand, the wonderfully warm, fuzzy feeling still spread all over him and he sometimes had to look away—wondering if God approved of such strong, passionate sensations. Would this be another sin he'd have to explain someday?

Harriet shielded her eyes from the late day sun and waved as Eli rode up. "Hello, Harri—How was business today?" he called to her.

"Not many customers, but nice of you to ask Rev. Marsh. How was the ministering today?" Harriet teased back.

Eli climbed off Gray, stretched his legs and back, and nodded to Morgan and Ford who had come out of the barn to take the horse. "He's had a long ride today, fellas. Give him extra oats tonight and a good rub," Eli said, smiling tiredly and turning to Harriet. "My dear, I am much better at burying the old than I am the young ones. So I guess today was a good ministering day for me. The whole town of Afton, or what's left of it, came out to say goodbye to George. He was a good man who lived a long life. His wife Daisy isn't well either. I don't think she'll last too long without George. It would have been a comfort to her if you had come with me," he said, glancing at Harriet, but she looked away.

"I can't go to every funeral with you Eli. Sometimes there are two or three a week with this War. You are gone all the time, and Rice and I are doing the best we can to keep things going here," she replied defensively.

Expecting this sort of answer from her, Eli just nodded his head. He was too tired and sore to get into their continuing debate about his demands as a minister and the usual duties of a minister's wife—very few of which Harri liked to perform. Arguing about it was an exhausting waste of time. And so he accepted that she preferred running her own business to being his pastoral partner. After all, it was her inheritance of the Limestone store and their house and farm that allowed them to live far more comfortably than they could have on his minimal minister's salary. He also couldn't complain too much because Harri fully supported him in the other love of his life which he knew he couldn't live without—breeding and raising horses. "Let's just call it a day and have supper," he murmured, putting his arm around her.

———

*2*

After supper, Eli and Rice sat on the side porch in Harri's cushioned wicker rockers, stretching their long legs and propping their feet on the railings. For Eli, the quiet of the evening was the best time of the summer day. The Smokey Mountain breezes cooled the day's heat, and the sweet smell of hay mixed with Harri's roses drifted through the wide porch that encircled the house. After sunset, the sky turned from pink to lilac before the stars lit the dark, indigo sky. It surprised no one that many people, Eli included, called this lush eastern corner of Tennessee, God's country. Eli could happily sit there all night drifting along. Rice, on the other hand, could not wait to continue the discussion of the Johnson horses. He had told Eli about Mack's offer over dinner. "So Pop, what do you think about those horses?" he asked.

Eli reached for his pipe and tobacco pouch. "How many do you think we are talking about, son?"

"Mack says he's got twenty horses and mules he can't take

care of. Two of the mares are going to foal in a few weeks too. I think we can get them for close to nothing because he just wants to find them a good home," Rice answered excitedly.

Eli whistled. "That's a lot more than I was thinking. That would bring us up to more than fifty horses. Could you and Morgan and Ford handle that many if I'm not here?"

Rice grinned. He knew his father was going to go for it. "The hardest work is getting them out to pasture in the morning and then back into the paddock and barn and bedded down at night. Besides, Morgan and Ford know lots of folks who need a little work for food or a place to sleep, if we run short," he said.

Eli frowned. "Your mother is not going to go along with us bringing on strange help. You know how she feels about that. There are just so many runaways and deserters roaming around. They'd likely be more trouble than they're worth."

"I think we should do it, Pop. The Johnsons' horses are some of the best around, besides ours of course. This is an amazing opportunity. We'll find reliable help if we need it. Mack is so troubled over losing Harold and Jimmy, there's no telling what he might do. I mean, what if he just starts putting them down?" Rice asked.

Alarmed, Eli stared at Rice. It was crushing to think of losing your children. Some people literally just lost their minds. Was this what was happening with Mack Johnson, he wondered. What would he do if he suddenly lost Rice forever? Would he lose all faith and sensibility? Exhaling, he said, "All right, there's so little comfort we can offer the Johnsons. The least we can do is try to save their horses. Let's go over and take a look tomorrow morning."

"Good," Rice said, standing up. "We can find a way. You'll see."

"One more thing," Eli sighed. "We'll need to start thinking about a bigger barn before the weather turns cold. I can't see any way around it."

Rice stretched his good arm out. "Can we worry about a bigger barn later, Pop? I need to ride over to see Lelia before it gets too dark. Tell Mother I won't be late," he said, hurrying down the steps.

Eli smiled. Lelia Patton was a few years younger than Rice, but she seemed to have become a special part of his life lately. The Pattons were a fine family, even though they tended to side with the Confederacy. Eli disagreed with them on that, but he couldn't blame them for their leanings. They were one of the few families around with a very large farm that had traditionally used slave labor to run the place. Most folks, if they could afford it, only used the blacks for housework, or they hired freed slaves like Morgan and Ford as permanent workers. Very few owned slaves. Still, Lelia would be a wonderful match for Rice, and he and Harri hoped she would be the one.

———

3

*June 2, 1863*
*Saw no soldiers at all yesterday on the trip to Afton. Surely,*
*God was watching out. Rice and I are going to take a look*
*at M. Johnson's horses today. I can't imagine where we'll*
*put them, but we have to try to help.*

The Johnson place was just a couple of miles up the road
toward Jonesborough. Rice and Eli got there quickly, seeing only a
handful of people on the road and no soldiers. A long dirt drive led
to the big white farmhouse, set back a few hundred yards from the
road on a hill in a grove of red maples. When they got closer to the
house, they could see that the front door was wide open. They went
up the steps to the porch and called and knocked. But neither Mack

nor his wife Mary or Nerva, their housekeeper, answered. So they went on down toward the barn. Although it was late morning and the air was hot and still, the barn doors were closed and bolted. No horses were in the paddock or the pastures.

The Johnson barn was a towering, horseshoe shaped structure with stalls ringing both sides of the walls all the way around. Even from a distance, they could hear the horses whinnying loudly, and stomping and kicking at the wood. Rice hurried ahead. "Something's not right, Pop," he yelled over his shoulder.

Eli felt a shiver down his back. "Wait for me Rice, let's go in together." It took both of them to remove the heavy wooden board which had been wedged through the door handles. When they swung open the big, wide doors, they were forced back by a rush of hot air. A powerful acrid stench of urine, manure and sweat stung their eyes and noses. Groping for his handkerchief, Eli angrily growled, "Merciful heavens—how long have these animals been shut up in here! Rice, quick get water into the troughs in the paddock. Let's get them out of here."

While Rice ran to the paddock to pump water, Eli took a deep breath, held the handkerchief tightly to his mouth and nose and stepped into the barn. His idea was to get to the back of the barn and open the doors there to get the air circulating. The noise around him was deafening. All the horses were jumping and shrieking at the sight of him. "God, just let me get to the back of the barn before one of these crazed animals kicks through its gate," he prayed. The deeper he walked into the barn, the worse the smell became, now mixing with a putrid rotting odor that filled his nose and throat, gagging him and forcing him to pant in order to breathe. By the time he reached the back doors, he was drenched in sweat and tears poured down his face. With the last of his strength he pushed open the heavy doors and gasped in the fresh air. Black dots danced in his stinging eyes and his whole body tingled. Legs buckling, he felt wet and numb and then the slipping down into black nothingness.

"Pop! Pop!—hold on!" Rice's voice crept into Eli's darkness. A cool cloth passed over his face and hands again and again until finally he was able to sit up with Rice's help. "Pop, I need you to move outside so you're not blocking the doorway. We can prop you up in the shade back there. You'll feel better outside. Then I can let the horses out into the pastures."

Rice's voice sounded so far away, but Eli struggled to do as he asked. He pulled and tugged his body outside and lay there as Rice slowly opened the gates to the stalls one by one. Two or three at a time, the horses madly rushed past, raising a thick cloud of body heat and dust. Some jostled at the water troughs, while others galloped wildly to the streams in the pastures. Wheezing and coughing, Rice finally appeared behind the last horses and sank down beside Eli. "There's still a Chestnut and a Black down in their stalls. They can't seem to get up. I can try to get some water in them, but they don't look good. How do you feel Pop?" he panted.

"Better now. I'm not sure what happened, but I felt like I was glimpsing the other side for sure," Eli chuckled weakly.

Rice gripped Eli's arm with his good hand. "Pop—back there in the barn," he stopped, his voice trembling.

"What is it?" Eli asked, sitting up straighter.

"It's Mack and Mary, Pop. They're hanging in there side by side from one of the beams," he said, lowering his head down. "Looks like they've been there for a while."

Unable to believe what he was hearing, Eli sat completely still staring at Rice. Slowly he pushed himself up on his feet and stood for a moment getting his balance back. His head felt a little light, but he could walk and the tingling sensation had passed. "Show me this," he said, turning back into the barn.

With all the doors open, a strong breeze had quickly cleared the air in the barn. The stalls were still unbearably mucked, but Rice and Eli had no trouble walking to the back right corner of the U-shaped barn. Just as Rice had described, Mack and Mary Johnson were hanging together, but of course, they looked nothing like the couple Eli had known for more than twenty years. Hands tied, their faces were swollen dark purple and distorted and their bodies were hardened. Flies swarmed on them in the heavy heat, speeding up the already visible decomposition.

"How could this be?" Eli finally managed to ask. "How could this be?"

"What do we do, Pop?" Rice asked quietly.

Looking away, Eli tried to think and steady himself from the shock. "We'll need to get Sheriff Hawkins over from Greeneville. I don't imagine he'll be able to get here before tomorrow. So I think we should at least cut them down and get them covered. They're already deteriorating so badly, we'll need to bury them as soon as the sheriff gets a look," he said shaking his head.

Searching around for a ladder, Rice asked, "Who do you think would do this Pop?"

"Nothing like this has ever happened around here. I can't imagine it was anyone we know," Eli answered. "Mack and Mary always kept to themselves, but most folks admired them for their selflessness in helping out with the abolitionist movement. Of course, they haven't been themselves at all since the boys died, but how do you explain this kind of violence?" he wondered.

Rice dragged a ladder over and propped it close to the bodies. "Pop, will you cut them down? I don't think I can do it," he said.

"It's okay, son," Eli said, pulling out his pocket knife and starting up the ladder. "You just lean against the ladder and steady it for me. Don't look at them either. It'll be a terrible sight when they drop," he warned.

It took many sawing strikes with the knife to chew through the thick ropes. Mack's body fell first, hitting the straw on the barn floor with a heavy thud. Mary's noose was even more difficult to cut through, but she finally dropped down on top of Mack, and Eli climbed down. The smell of death and human waste oozing out of their failed organs overwhelmed both men. Gagging, they turned away and rushed outside into the fresh air. At last breathing normally, Eli said, "We have to go back in there and straighten them out and cover them at least."

"They're such a mess, Pop. I don't know if I can touch them. Can't we just throw some blankets over them?" Rice asked.

"In all my years tending to the dead, this is the worst I've ever seen," Eli said wearily. "These nice people so violated beyond reason. I guess we've been lucky not to have seen bodies like this on the battlefields. I've heard that the burial details are told to 'Plant them where they fall' because the bodies are just too gruesome to move and literally breaking apart."

"It's too much to take in. I was just talking to Mack yesterday about the horses," Rice said, his voice cracking.

Eli stood up and tied his handkerchief over his nose and mouth. "I'm going to stretch them out properly and cover them up. It will be faster if you help me, but I understand if you can't," he said, touching Rice on the shoulder. Rice said nothing, but took a deep breath, covered his face and followed Eli back to the bodies. It didn't take long for them to lay out Mack and Mary's stiffening remains side by side on the barn floor. Eli gently covered them with some of the loose horse blankets and then said simply, "You're in a far better place now old friends. God be with you and rest your weary souls."

Outside, washing off at the pump, Rice looked at his father. "Do you think someone might have followed Mack home from our place or was here waiting for him when he got home?"

Eli looked around nervously. Rice's suggestion that whoever did this might have been lurking around their house or the Bee and then followed Mack home was terrifying. Suddenly he felt afraid for Harri. She spent so much time alone in the store and at the house. Up until now he hadn't worried about her. But now a panicky feeling came over him. "Rice, I want you to ride back home right away.

Check on your Mother and tell her what's happened. Then ride on over to Greeneville and get the sheriff. You'll need to tell him when you saw Mack yesterday. It might help him find out who did this."

Rice heard the change in his father's voice. What if something had happened to his Mother while they were gone? He turned and walked quickly to his horse. "Don't worry Pop. I can do all of this. I'll be back tomorrow with Sheriff Hawkins. Will you be okay here by yourself?"

"I'll be all right," Eli said quietly. "One more thing—before you leave for Greeneville, find Morgan and Ford. I may need some help here. Ask Ford to ride over right away and tell Morgan to stay close by your Mother. She'll have to help him bed down the horses tonight," he added.

"Okay Pop, see you tomorrow. Try not to worry. "

Eli shrugged. "I'm going to check the house. Maybe Nerva is hiding in there somewhere scared to death. We forgot about her didn't we?"

Rice nodded. "Maybe she got away."

"Maybe so," Eli said, giving Rice a hug. "Be careful son. Keep your eyes wide open and get a fresh horse at home. Ride as fast as you can, but try not to look suspicious if you run into soldiers or strangers. Maybe you'll make it to Greeneville before dark."

As Rice started to ride away, Eli shouted, "Tell your Mother I'll see her tomorrow."

Rice waved his short arm over his head and galloped down the drive to the road. Eli watched him until he was out of sight and then walked toward the house praying silently, "Dear Lord, protect Rice and Harri. Please don't let anything happen to them." Shaking his head, he thought his prayer sounded like a child's, not a seasoned minister who helped people pray every day, but he didn't care. "Please hear me on this one," he said out loud as he climbed the steps to the house.

---

4

Leaving his father alone at the Johnsons' was frightening, but Rice truly felt relieved to be getting away from all the horror. Embarrassed that he had reacted badly to the dead bodies, he now felt empowered to be riding away to check on his mother and then on to find the sheriff. His father was right of course. All of his friends who had gone off to war had already seen this kind of horrible death over and over. He vowed to be stronger from now on.

Thankfully, he saw no one on the road and he reached the Bee in no time. Inside, Harriet was standing at the counter scooping hard candy into a bag. "Mother, are you all right?" he asked breathing hard.

Harriet looked up surprised. "I'm fine. Something wrong?"

Rice glanced around the store. His Uncle Will Burkhart and his little cousin David were looking at clothes in the back. Rice waved to them and said quietly, "Mother, I need to talk to you."

Harriet looked at Rice's face. It was drawn and tight. Suddenly, her baby looked old to her. She wondered if something had happened to Eli, but instead of asking, she simply called to her brother, "Will, we're going outside for a minute. There's candy here for David."

In the late afternoon sun, Rice told his mother what he and Eli had found at the Johnsons'. "Pop's staying over there tonight, and I'm going to ride to Greeneville to get the sheriff," he finished.

Harriet sank down on the bench by the door looking small and fragile to Rice. Her hair was pulled back in a tight bun accenting the lines and wrinkles on her face. Crying softly, she dabbed her eyes with her lace handkerchief.

"Mother, have any strangers been here today?" Rice asked, taking her hand.

Harriet sobbed and gulped for a breath. "A Union soldier was here. He's looking for horses. He seemed to know about your father and our horses. He wondered if your father might be interested in some trading. He left this," she said, pulling a folded paper from her pocket and handing it to Rice

"Huh—wonder what Pop will think of this," Rice said, taking his hat off and running his fingers through his dark curly hair as he

read the notice. "What would the army want to trade back to us for good horses?"

Harriet noticed that dirt had crusted under Rice's hat band leaving a dark ring around his forehead, but she said nothing about his appearance. She was so relieved that he was here talking to her and that Eli was safe for now. "Hopefully, that soldier won't come back at all," she sighed as she stood up. "The Johnsons were such kind people. I don't understand how something like this could happen. Who would do such a thing?"

"I don't know Mother. But now we know, no one around here is safe. If it happened to them, we could be next," Rice warned, looking away from her as he tried to shake off the memory of the dangling bodies. "I've got to get going to Greeneville. Will you be all right here?"

Harriet straightened her dress and smoothed her hair. "Of course I will."

"Pop wants Ford to ride over and help him. Morgan will be here with you though. You'll have to help him get the horses in. Pop wants him to guard the house tonight. Please let him Mother," he pleaded.

"I won't be doing any sleeping until you and your father are back home. So I guess Morgan and I will just watch each other all night." Harriet sniffed and walked back into the store. She needed to tell her brother this news, so he could get on home to his wife Betsy and their other children. No one should be alone now.

Rice walked his horse over to the barn, located Ford and Morgan and told them what Eli wanted. "Load up one of my shotguns Morgan and keep it with you. Don't let Mother talk you into putting it aside. Just stay on the front porch tonight and tomorrow watch the store. Pop and I will be back as soon as we can," he promised. Quickly, they saddled two fresh horses. Ford rode off first, worrying that he might get stopped or picked off for being a black man on the loose. He figured the chance to explain his free status might not even come up and he would be a goner. Rice followed behind him, waving to Harriet who was standing outside the Bee with Will and David. She put her fingers to her lips in a silent kiss.

———

5

Eli opened the big screen door on the front porch and walked into the Johnsons' silent house. The dense shade from the grove of maples kept the temperature much cooler inside and with all the windows open, a constant breeze moved the air. Such a wonderful home, he thought, remembering all the mischief and fun when the boys were little and running about. "All gone now," he whispered. "All of them resting together for eternity." I'm intruding on their peace, he thought, his boots clicking too loudly on the polished floors as he moved through the house. The parlor and the dining rooms looked perfectly normal—all neatly arranged, nothing out of place. He paused to look at dim pictures of Harold and Jimmy draped in black on the mantelpiece.

The kitchen area was a different matter. Clearly something violent had happened there. The table and chairs were turned over at jagged angles with broken dishes strewn about. A pot of uncooked potatoes sat on the cold wood stove. The back screen door had been knocked off its hinges. Dried blood and clumps of hair clung to the back steps. Torn bits of black and white fabric were snagged on the bottom step. Eli tried to remember what Mary had been wearing, because it looked like whoever did this had surprised her in the kitchen. To the side of the back door, he opened another door which he assumed was to a pantry, but instead he found himself in a tiny bedroom. He guessed this was Nerva's quarters. It had been torn apart too, with drawers dumped out, mattress pulled up, and clothing pulled from the closet. "What could they have been looking for in here?" Eli muttered, but he couldn't begin to imagine.

Retracing his steps to the front hallway, he went up the stairs to the second floor. Again and again his heavy boots echoed eerily through the house. He had been in this home many times over the past years, but he had never had a reason to visit the upstairs. Not surprisingly, it looked very similar to his own home, with a master bedroom at the head of the stairs and three other bedrooms lining the hallway. Nothing was amiss and there was no sign of Nerva either. All the beds were neatly made, chamber pots emptied, washstand pitchers filled, clean towels and soap ready. It appeared that the intruders hadn't bothered with the upstairs at all.

Back downstairs, Eli sat on the front porch to wait for Ford. He imagined that Rice had already made it home and gone on to Greeneville. He worried about Harri's reaction to this terrible news. She was strong, but she generally didn't do well in abnormal situations. That's why she preferred not to get too involved with other people outside the family. Over the years, they had socialized more with the Johnsons than most others, because Rice and the boys were such good friends. But when Harold and Jimmy were conscripted into the Confederate army, Mack and Mary closed themselves off from the rest of the community. Instead of trying to reach out and comfort them, Harri stayed completely away and made no attempt to see them. He had continued to look in on them, but mostly talked horses with Mack. When the news came that the boys had died and been buried in Mississippi, he had arranged a memorial service at their little church. Harri had gone to the service and taken food back to the house afterwards and sat with Mary. But she had not been back since, because it was just easier to stay away. How would she deal with this he wondered?

Closing his eyes, Eli dozed off for a bit, but the creaking sounds of the empty house kept jerking him awake. He jumped up when he heard the sound of a horse on the drive and with great relief he recognized Ford trotting toward the house. Shaking himself to calm his nerves, he went down the steps to meet him. "Thanks for coming," he said as Ford climbed off his horse. "Any trouble?"

Ford's shirt was soaked through with sweat and his dark muscular body glistened in the sunlight. His eyes were big and wide and flicking back and forth. "I be terrible scared the whole way Reverend suh," he said hoarsely. "Stayed off the road in the woods as much as I could. Still I keep feelin' somebody followin' me."

Eli nervously looked back down the drive, but saw no one. "You did a good job, Ford, and you're all right now. Go on over to the pump and cool off a bit. We've got a lot of work to do," he said patting him on the back.

After a long drink of water, Ford rinsed off and mopped his face and hands with a rag. He was still looking about uneasily, but he seemed a bit calmer. "Mistah Rice say there be trouble over here. Where Mistah Johnson, Reverend suh?" he asked.

Eli stared at Ford, realizing now that Rice had decided not to tell him about the Johnsons. Seeing how frightened Ford was just riding over here alone, Eli shook his head and marveled at how wise Rice had become. "Let's sit down on the porch steps here, Ford. I have something to tell you," Eli said, walking back towards the house.

"Look, there's no good way of saying this," Eli said. "Something terrible has happened here. Rice and I found the Johnsons hanged to death in the barn."

Ford started to tremble. "Hanged—you mean kilt, suh?"

"Yes, killed. It's not possible they could have done that to themselves. The barn was shut up tight and bolted from the outside with all the horses still in their stalls. Rice and I got the horses out into the pasture and we cut the bodies down and covered them. They're still in the barn. That's why Rice has gone to get the sheriff," he answered.

"Reverend suh, what you need me for?" Ford asked shakily.

Eli had no idea what Ford had seen or suffered through, growing up as a slave on a Mississippi cotton plantation. But the news of the hangings seemed to have brought back memories that terrified him. "I need you to help me with the horses before it gets dark. You don't have to go into the barn. We'll just put them in the paddock for the night and feed them as best we can there. Rice filled the troughs before he left," Eli said, looking at the sky. "I don't think it will rain tonight, so they'll be all right."

Relieved a bit, Ford nodded and walked toward the paddock. Work made him feel less afraid. If he kept on moving, maybe the evil in this place would miss him this time. "How many horses, Reverend suh?" he asked.

"I think about eighteen. There's two more that never made it out of the barn. I'll check on them now," Eli said.

The air in the barn had cleared thanks to the abundant cross-breezes created by the impressive horseshoe design. He wondered how hard it would be to enlarge his barn in a similar manner and he began to draft out a plan in his mind. He was surprised at himself for feeling hopeful about the future in the midst of all the misery surrounding him. Reaching the Chestnut's stall first, he found the beautiful mare still lying on her side, breathing more easily. Eli spoke soothingly to her and gently stroked her long neck. She was able to swallow the water he carefully squeezed into her mouth. Even with these small improvements though, the horse would have to get up soon or her intestines would become blocked, bringing on a slow excruciating death. Then he would have to put her down.

Moving on to another stall, he found that the Black had already died. Sadly, he covered him with blankets to try to discourage the fly infestation. It would be another day or two until they could hoist this body out of the stall, and they would need at least three men to do it. His earlier hopefulness vanished, and he felt the heavy weight of being depressingly old and tired. He wanted nothing more than to be home with Harri and away from this responsibility, but he forced himself to the back of the barn to check on the Johnsons. Their bodies lay just as he had left them earlier. Except for their rotting odor, they seemed to be resting peacefully. He was glad that he and Rice had gotten them down and laid them out, but he worried that the rapid rate of decay was going to be a problem in moving them to the cemetery. He wished he had thought to tell Rice to ask Herm, the church handyman, to make two coffins and bring them over. It would be much better to move them that way. "Rest easy—we'll get you out of here tomorrow," he whispered. Then he collected feed buckets and grain sacks and began the first of many trips of carrying them out to the paddock.

Ford had worked steadily while Eli was in the barn. Piles of hay lined the rails inside the fencing, and the water troughs were over-flowing. He filled the feed buckets with the grain and hung them all around the paddock. "Great job, Ford," Eli said, mopping his face. "I think we can start bringing the horses in pretty soon. It won't be dark for a few more hours."

Ford shielded his eyes and looked out into the pasture. "Some of 'em be way out, Reverend suh."

"Well, we'll just have to ride out there and drive them in like we do at home. Let's do that now," Eli said, walking towards Gray. It took a good hour to round up the horses and get them back into the paddock and secured for the night. Then of course they jostled and kicked about and couldn't settle down in the close confinement.

"They be okay Reverend suh, once they find the feed and water. They smart," Ford shouted over the deafening horse noise. "Let's leave 'em be."

Eli stared at the crowded paddock. "I hope you're right," he shouted back and walked to the pump to wash the dust off his hands and face. When Ford joined him, Eli asked quietly, "Did Rice leave for Greeneville before you?"

"We leave 'round the same time, Reverend suh," he answered.

"So he should be almost there by now," Eli said more to himself than to Ford.

Ford smiled for the first time. "He be ridin' one of your fast horses, so he most likely there."

Eli cleared his throat. "Ford, do you know Nerva?"

"Yassuh, I know her. Where she be?" he asked, looking around.

"I was hoping you could help me with that. She's not here as far as I can tell. She might have seen something. Where would she hide?" Eli asked.

Ford shifted around nervously. "Maybe she in the tunnel," he whispered.

Eli stared at Ford. "What? What tunnel?" He thought he knew of the few secret tunnels in the area. They had been used for several years to help shuttle desperate souls to the North. But he had never heard of one on the Johnson property.

Ford stared back at Eli. "There be one here, I swear Reverend suh, and Morgan knows about it too."

"Show me where it is Ford," Eli demanded.

"I don't know exactly. I never been in it," Ford apologized. "But I heared talk that the Johnsons helped out a lot of peoples."

For the second time that day, Eli couldn't believe what he was hearing. How could he not have known that Mack and Mary and probably the boys were part of the Underground Railroad? Could this secret, passionate activity be why they were so brutally murdered, or was it just a random act by strangers he wondered?

Ford looked at Eli nervously. "I'm sorry I don't know where it is, Reverend, suh," he stammered.

"It's all right Ford. Let's go up to the house and see if we can find something to eat. I haven't eaten since early this morning. Then we'll have a look around and see if we can find this tunnel," Eli said.

Ford hung back. "I don't know about that house, Reverend suh. There be an evil feelin' here. We be safer outside," he said hoarsely.

"Suit yourself. I'll go see what I can find and bring it out to the porch," Eli said patiently. It was no use trying to deal with superstitions now. "You call me if you see anyone."

Ford followed him up to the porch and watched Eli disappear into the house. Feeling miserably afraid, he crouched tentatively on the steps. He didn't want to be left alone, but this house of the newly dead terrified him, especially the dead who were still lying on the barn floor.

Eli went directly to the kitchen and picked his way through the mess. On a wooden cutting board, he found loaves of stale bread under a towel and a jar of honey. Thinking this would do nicely, he hurried back outside to Ford who hadn't moved an inch. "I ain't seen nothin', Reverend suh," he said, gratefully taking some bread and honey. Eli sat down next to him and they ate in silence.

"Much better," Eli finally said, licking his fingers. "I need to wash off this stickiness and then I'm going to have a look around for this tunnel. If Nerva is in there, it's important that we find her as soon as we can." Ford followed closely behind Eli and washed his hands off too and then stayed by his side as Eli walked around the side of the big house. Lattice was tightly nailed under the porch with no opening to the crawlspace underneath. As they moved towards the back, they saw no cellar doors. The rear of the house faced a wide back yard with an outhouse off to one side and a silent chicken coop on the other side. A large vegetable garden stretched back about fifty yards ending with thick rows of corn and then dense woods behind.

"Those poor chickens—I can't imagine they're still alive after being closed up for two days in this heat with no fresh feed or water," Eli said. He felt annoyed with himself that he hadn't thought to look for other farm animals besides the horses.

Ford didn't answer, and when Eli turned and looked at him, he found him staring at the bloody back steps and the busted screen door. "That look awful mean, Reverend suh," he said quietly and then, "Look, there a rut cella door unda the steps."

"Here, let's get that open and see what's down there before it starts getting too dark," Eli said, grabbing the ring and pulling the slanted door up until it rested against the house. A blast of cool earthy air hit their faces. Eli took some matches from his pocket and struck one to help see inside. Ford stood back not wanting to descend into the blackness while Eli climbed in. Right away he found a lantern on the second step. Lighting it, he was able to easily walk down six wide steps to a smooth dirt floor. Barrels of onions, potatoes, carrots, and turnips lined the dirt walls. Above them were shelves loaded with canned jars of tomatoes, pickled beans, cucumbers, corn, and sugared apples, peaches, jams and jellies. Eli smiled to himself picturing Mary and Nerva, working side by side in the kitchen above, putting up these specialties for winter.

"Reverend suh?" Ford called down the steps.

"I'm all right," Eli shouted back. "There's nothing unusual down here so far. I'm going to go around to the other side. I can see steps coming down from inside the house over there."

"It gettin' dark fast now, suh. Won't you come on back out where's I can see you?" Ford called back.

Hearing the trembling in Ford's voice, Eli turned around. He couldn't risk the chance that Ford might run off to hide. He could finish looking around the cellar in the morning, but before he climbed out, he called quietly, "Nerva, it's Reverend Marsh. Are you in here? Your friend Ford is here with me too. I know you're afraid, but we can help you. It's okay to come on out now." He strained to hear any sound or movement, but only heard silence. He turned and climbed up the steps to find Ford crouching at the top. "If Nerva's down there, she's not answering," Eli said, handing Ford the lantern. "And

I didn't find any tunnel yet either," he added, closing the cellar door.

With darkness falling rapidly, they made their way back around to the front porch with the help of the lantern. "There are parlor lamps just inside," Eli said, positioning Ford against the open front door. "Stand here and shine the light inside for me so I can find them." Not waiting for Ford to refuse, Eli hurried into the house and came back out in less than a minute with two lamps which he lit right away, flooding the porch with yellow light. "Now Ford I'm going to go back inside and look for some blankets. We can sleep right here in these porch chairs if you like. You wait right here, all right." Eli said, placing his hand on Ford's arm.

"Please just hurry Reverend suh," Ford whispered, as if someone else might be listening.

Taking one of the lamps, Eli turned back inside and hurried to the upstairs. Quickly he grabbed quilts and pillows from the boys' beds. He didn't think anyone would mind, and who was going to use them now anyway? This family simply didn't exist anymore at least in this world. Back on the porch, he found Ford crouched on the top step. Eli handed him a quilt and pillow, and Ford sank down on the floor, pulling the quilt tightly around him, saying "Thank you, Reverend suh."

Eli pulled two of the big rocking chairs together and sat down at last. He pulled off his boots and loosened his collar and string tie. Putting his feet up, he stretched out between the chairs and pulled out his pipe and tobacco and sat quietly smoking for a bit. Ford lay still and seemed to have nodded off to sleep. Eli was too worried about Harri and Rice and the shocking deaths of Mack and Mary to let himself sleep. To pass the time, he pulled out his diary.

June 2, 1863 Evening
Rice and I rode to the Johnsons' this morning to make an offer on their horses and start moving them over to our place right away. Instead we found Mack and Mary dead, hanging in the barn probably since yesterday. Horses were in a frantic state and Nerva is missing. Rice rode home to tell Harri and send Ford back to help me. He's gone on to Greeneville to get Sheriff Hawkins. Ford got here all right, but he's scared to death and won't go near the barn where the bodies are. He thinks the Johnsons have a secret tunnel here and maybe that's where Nerva is or how she got away. I haven't found it, but I'll keep looking. If it's true and Mack and Mary were part of the Underground Railway, they might have been killed by Confederate sympathizers. Right now there's no other sign of who might have done this. It doesn't look like robbery—nothing seems to be missing from the house. Tomorrow can't come soon enough. I just want to go home to Harri.

---

*6*

At dawn, the horses began stirring and whinnying in the cramped paddock. Eli opened his eyes, surprised that he had fallen asleep. He willed his stiffened muscles to let his body get up out of the chairs. God—how everything ached and his head throbbed. The thick smell of the burned down kerosene lamps clogged his throat. He needed water right away and he hoped he could find coffee in the kitchen. Ford, on the other hand, looked very peaceful, still rolled up in the quilt just as he had been the night before. Hearing Eli putting on his boots, he sat up and scratched his head. "I guess you's right Reverend suh, the Lord still watchin afta us," he yawned.

Eli stood up. "He always does Ford, even when it doesn't seem like it. I'm going to try the outhouse in the back and then see if I can make us some breakfast," Eli said, going down the steps and around the house. "You could start letting the horses out into the pasture when you're awake."

Ford sat staring out across the fields. He needed to piss in the worst way. Normally he would have gone behind the barn, but he couldn't go near there, not with the dead still lying inside. He wished he was back safe at the Marsh barn. He stood up and headed down toward the paddock just as Eli came back around the house, carrying eggs. "I checked the coop. Some of the chickens seem to have made it. They're angry and hungry, but not too bad, and there are lots of eggs. There's nothing wrong back there Ford. You should use the outhouse if you need to," Eli said motioning with his head.

"Thank you Reverend suh," Ford answered, hurrying to the back.

While Eli busied himself with breakfast, Ford got to work with the horses. After breakfast, Eli offered to help with getting the rest of the horses out, but Ford insisted that he didn't need him. "Fine then," Eli said. "I'm going to look for that tunnel."

Back inside the house, Eli looked all around the dining room, kitchen and the back porch. Why couldn't he find the inside entrance to the cellar? It didn't make any sense. He had clearly seen steps coming down to the cellar from the main floor, and most houses had the entrance to the cellar near the kitchen to make it easy to bring up the stored food. The only place left was Nerva's tiny room which was still a chaos of overturned furniture and clothing. Wedging himself inside and pushing the door closed, he scanned the walls and the flooring he could see. He laughed to himself when he realized he was looking at a door in the floor—behind the room door—not visible unless the room door was closed. A mirror was propped beside it which Eli guessed was supposed to be over the door to conceal it even more. Ford could be right about a secret tunnel he thought, because this was a very unusual location for a cellar door. Excited to have found it, he moved the debris away and pulled open the door with the small hatch ring. Cool earthy air filled his nose, and he could see wooden steps descending into darkness below. Not seeing any lanterns this time, Eli hurried back out to the front porch to get one of the lights from the night before.

Seeing that Ford had just released the last of the horses into the pasture, Eli motioned for him to come up to the house. As Ford walked towards him, Eli gazed at the horses galloping happily in the green grass. Their chestnut, black, and silvery white colors danced in the sunlight. These were gloriously beautiful animals, all carefully handpicked by Mack. There was no doubt in Eli's mind that he and Rice were doing the right thing by preserving this herd.

"They be all right today, Reverend suh," Ford said, squinting into the sun.

"They certainly seem to be. Excellent work Ford," Eli agreed, putting his hand on Ford's shoulder. "I found the inside cellar door. It's in Nerva's room, kinda out of sight, so you may be right. Go around back and pull open the outside door again to throw some light in there. I'll take a lantern down with me from the inside."

As he lit the lantern and started down the steps, Eli could hear Ford opening up the cellar from the outside. To his surprise when he got to the bottom of the steps, the light from the outside door was barely visible from where he stood. Bags of flour and corn meal were piled up on tables and jugs of cider lined the shelves. Eli walked to the end of this space looking for the tunnel opening and turned to the right where he could see the light from the outside door shining brightly. He was just climbing the outside steps when Ford called, "I hear riders!"

"It's probably Rice and Sheriff Hawkins," Eli said, reaching the outside and motioning to Ford to follow him around to the front of the house. Heart pounding, he hurried out to the drive just as Rice with the sheriff and two other men rode up to the house."Everything all right, Pop?" Rice asked, jumping off his horse.

"Yes, thank God!" Eli answered, hugging Rice and then turning to Sheriff Hawkins. "Thanks for coming."

"Morning Reverend Marsh," Hawkins said, shaking Eli's hand. "Rice here told us what's happened. This is George and Albert, two of my deputies. I thought we might need some extra help here this morning. The Johnsons still in the barn?"

Eli nodded. "They haven't been touched since we cut them down and covered them yesterday—terrible shock for Rice and me," he said, shaking his head as he led them down to the barn. Everyone followed except for Ford who headed over to the paddock.

"Who's that?" Hawkins asked, pointing to Ford. "Is he yours?"

Eli resented Hawkins' use of the word 'yours' which usually meant 'owned', but he calmly answered, "That's Ford. He works for me and rode over to help me out last night."

Silence settled over the group when they reached the covered bodies, and Hawkins pulled back the blankets to view the remains. The rapid decomposition had already changed their appearance significantly from the day before. He carefully examined the knotted ropes and then directed the deputies to cut them away from the bodies and bag them as evidence. "I think it's all right to go ahead and get these folks buried, Reverend," he said at last, pulling the blankets back over the bodies. "Let's go back out into the fresh air."

Outside in the bright sun, everyone breathed deeply trying to clear the overwhelming, sickening smell from their noses and throats. "Rice said Mack Johnson was over at your place day before yesterday in the morning. That right Reverend?" Hawkins asked.

Eli nodded his head. "I didn't see him because I was over in Afton attending to George Pickering's funeral. But yes, Rice said he came by to ask me about taking over his horses. He's been awfully down with Harold and Jimmy gone and he couldn't handle them any more. That's why Rice and I rode over yesterday to take a look and maybe start moving them to our place a few at a time."

"You still thinking of doing that?" Hawkins asked, staring at Eli.

"Definitely!" Rice broke in, not waiting for Eli to reply.

"There doesn't seem to be anyone else to take them," Eli said quietly, frowning at Rice. "We've known the Johnson family for years, and I think Mack's only living relative is his cousin Andrew, our esteemed military governor in Nashville. He used to have a small farm in Greeneville, but as I'm sure you know, it's been taken over by the

Confederates. There's no other family land here now that I know of."

"I know all about what happened to Andrew Johnson's place," Hawkins said. "His family isn't even in Greeneville right now. I think it would be okay for you to take the horses as soon as possible." Just as he finished saying this, George and Albert, who had been looking around the barn, rushed out.

"Sheriff, we found a Confederate cap on the other side of the barn near the back doors and there's more ropes back there too," George said.

Hawkins and Eli and Rice went back to take a look. The cap was lying in the dirt near the doors. Picking it up, Hawkins handed it to George. "Put this in with the ropes we're taking, but it may not mean anything."

Eli agreed. "I guess it's possible it might belong to one of the killers, but it could have been an extra one of Harold's or Jimmy's that just got left behind."

Hawkins and his men walked up to the house with Eli and Rice following. They looked through the rooms and the cellar and examined the blood and hair and torn fabric on the back steps. "It looks like that's where they got Mary and maybe Nerva, the housekeeper. She's still missing so far," Eli said.

"Most likely," Hawkins agreed. "So you're not aware of any enemies the Johnsons might have had?"

"None at all." Eli said quietly.

"What about this Nerva? She a Negro?" he asked.

"Yes. Her name is actually Minerva, but she goes by Nerva. She's worked for them since she was a young girl. She's probably in her twenties now," Eli answered. "I'm hoping she's just run off scared to death and will turn up," he finished. He decided not to mention Ford's idea about the tunnel, since he hadn't found it when he searched the cellar. Besides, it was a well-known fact that Hawkins did not approve of the Underground movement. News of another possible tunnel in the area might complicate matters and delay moving the horses.

"Well, if she does turn up, you'll let me know, so I can talk to her, won't you Reverend?" Hawkins said, walking around to the front of the house. "I think we've seen enough here. There's no telling who did this. Maybe soldiers, maybe not. I haven't heard of any other violence like this. If it's Confederates, they're taking a big risk. There are reports of Union soldiers in different parts of the area now too. War brings out the worst in folks sometimes, but the killing of private citizens for no apparent reason is a great concern."

"It's true, Pop," Rice said, rejoining the group. He had been helping Ford in the paddock while the house was searched. "I saw a group of Union soldiers just outside of Greeneville."

Eli shivered. He needed to know that Harri was safe. "Is something going on, Sheriff?"

Hawkins and his men were mounting their horses. "There's a rumor out there that the Union is going to make another run on Knoxville pretty soon. They want to free up the river and the railroad down there," he said.

"That'll be a fight," Eli sighed, thinking about all the dead and wounded men. "So it's all right if we get these folks buried properly now? I'd like to do it over at my church's cemetery."

"The sooner, the better. They certainly need to be laid to rest," Hawkins said, squinting down the drive at the sound of a wagon. "Who do you suppose that is?"

Eli shielded his eyes. "It looks like Herm, my church handyman," he said relieved. "Looks like he brought over some coffins."

Herm, a big, burly man with a red bandana tied around his long gray hair, smiled and waved at the group when he pulled up. "Miz Marsh said you'd be needing these, Reverend."

"So everything is all right at the house?" Eli asked, shaking Herm's hand.

"It seems so," Herm answered. "She said to tell you to get on home with Rice and Ford. She's tired of tending your horses!"

Eli laughed. "We'll do just that. Thanks for bringing these Herm," he said pointing at the coffins. "Drive on down to the barn and I'll be right there."

"You need help with that, Reverend?" Hawkins asked.

"I think we can manage, Sheriff. Thanks again for coming so quickly."

"Be careful on the road, Reverend, and around your place. Be sure someone is watching Mrs. Marsh in that store too. We just don't know who's out there. When you're in Greeneville next, stop in and see me. You too Rice," he called, as they rode away.

———

*7*

Eli looked at Rice. "How many horses do you think we can take today?"

"Ford thinks you and he can each trail two behind you easily. Now that we've got the wagon, we could probably tie two to that too," Rice said, rubbing his short arm. "I can't manage trailing horses, but I could probably drive the wagon, and Herm could ride my horse and trail two more."

"Eight horses would be a good start," Eli said smiling at Rice. "You and Ford go ahead and start rounding them up. We can put the others back into their stalls once Herm and I get Mack and Mary out of the barn," he added.

Then he hurried down to meet Herm who was already unloading the coffins. "Did Mrs. Marsh tell you what happened here?"

"Yes sir, she told me. It's terrible sad," Herm said, shaking his head.

"I've never seen anything like this. Prepare yourself," Eli said, tying his handkerchief around his face. Herm did the same, and together they carried the coffins deep into the barn where the bodies lay.

Herm had helped Eli with most of the church burials in recent years, but nothing had prepared him for the sight and condition of these bodies as they carefully lifted each one into the coffins. "My God, Reverend, who could have done this?" he gasped, struggling to breathe.

"I can't imagine," Eli panted, as he gently tucked the blankets around the bodies before they slid the lids into place. "But they are surely together in heaven and no one can hurt them again. At least we will be able to bury them here at the church among friends and not in some miserable battlefield like Harold and Jimmy." He sighed and looked away, thinking of the many bereft souls in shallow graves far away from home.

Unaccustomed to seeing Eli so dejected, Herm said, "I'll pull the wagon as close to the barn as I can, so we can get these folks loaded and start back."

Eli nodded and followed Herm out of the barn. Looking out to the pastures, he waved and motioned to Rice and Ford to ride in. It looked like they had already gotten most of the horses back into the paddock.

As Herm moved the wagon into position, Eli turned to Rice and Ford. "We're going to need your help getting the coffins into the wagon."

Ford backed away. "I be afraid of the dead, Reverend suh," he whispered.

"I know you are, Ford, but we'll all be with you, and these poor souls will be forever grateful for your helping hand. I imagine they'll kindly watch over you from now on," Eli said quietly.

Ford cocked his head and considered this idea. "Like angels, you mean suh?"

Eli smiled. "That's right—like angels."

"C'mon Ford. I'll be right next to you. It'll be easy," Rice added.

"I try," Ford mumbled.

"Good man," Eli said. "The sooner we do this, the sooner we can get on home."

Herm had already propped two boards up to the back of the wagon. "We can just slide them up on these," he said. And in a matter of minutes it was all over. Eli, Herm and Ford carried the coffins, and Rice secured them with ropes in the wagon so they wouldn't shift.

While Herm pulled the wagon up to the front of the house, Eli, Rice and Ford began hurriedly mucking out the horse stalls in the barn for the horses staying behind for the night. "What about the Chestnut that was down, Pop?' Rice asked.

"I haven't had a chance to check on her. I'm afraid she may be gone, but I'll go around and see," Eli said, feeling dejected that he might have lost another horse. But when he got around to the other side of the barn, he was overjoyed to see that the Chestnut was standing quietly in her stall. "Let's get you outside into the fresh air," he whispered, placing a loose rope around her neck. "She made it ," he called to Rice as he passed the barn doors. "We'll take her with us today."

By early afternoon they started the ride back home trailing eight horses and carrying the two coffins. They felt uneasy leaving the rest of the horses alone for the night, but there was no other solution. "We'll hurry back early tomorrow," Eli assured Rice. With one last look around, they started out the drive to the road. "If Nerva is hiding here, she's going to be alone now," he said, shaking his head.

"She gone, Reverend suh," Ford whispered.

———

8

Harriet walked across the road to open the Bee after helping Morgan turn the horses out. Although she was good at the barn work, she hated it and generally stayed away from horse chores unless she was needed like this morning. Eli and Rice were mystified that she didn't share their passion for the horses and instead only viewed them as a way to get around. How strange it felt, being home without either of them. Eli had always had a strict rule that if he was away, Rice had to be home. Last night was the first time she had been completely alone in the house in years, and every sound made her jump even with Morgan stationed on the front porch.

As hard as she tried to push away the dark dangerous fears, she couldn't help but wonder if something had already happened to Eli and Rice. And then those soldiers stopping by yesterday looking for Eli didn't help at all. They were polite, but it was uncomfortable the way they were looking around. She hoped Eli wouldn't have anything to do with trading with them. It made her mad just thinking about it. He was a Presbyterian minister after all, not a horse trader. "The very idea is ridiculous!" she muttered, as she unlocked the Bee. Just as she was pushing the door open, she saw something moving in the bushes beside the store. "Who's there?" she screamed.

Morgan, who had been watching her from the barn, streaked across the road carrying Rice's rifle. "What, Miz Marsh?" he shouted.

"There's something in there!" she cried, pointing to the bushes.

Morgan cocked the rifle and walked toward the bushes. As he rounded the corner of the store, he saw bloody, brown legs stretched across the ground. Pulling back the bushes and kneeling down, he said, "Nerva, that you?"

"Who is it?" Harriet called out.

Morgan leaned his rifle against the wall and stuck his head around the corner of the store. "Nerva, from the Johnsons' is back there on the ground."

Harriet hurried over to look as Morgan pulled Nerva's battered body from under the bushes. "Is she breathing?"

Morgan listened to Nerva's chest. "Her heart beatin'. I'll get some water," he said, running to the water pump in front of the store.

Harriet knelt down beside Nerva and took out her handkerchief. She gently brushed some of the dirt and twigs from the cuts on her swollen face and matted hair. Deep gashes and bruises ringed her arms, hands, legs and feet, and she was covered in bug bites. Her dress was in shreds and she had no shoes. How did she manage to get all the way over here like this, Harriet wondered.

When Morgan came back with the water, Harriet brought out towels and wash cloths from the store, and together they cleaned Nerva up enough to move her inside the Bee. Harriet spread a sheet and pillow on one of the benches over by the shoes and they laid her down. Still Nerva showed no sign of regaining consciousness, even as Harriet kept placing cool cloths on her head and rubbing her wrists. "Maybe she hurt inside too," Morgan said.

"It's possible," Harriet agreed. "Or maybe she is just completely exhausted and in shock. Let's give her a little more time."

Morgan shook his head. "Why she run away like that?"

Harriet looked up at Morgan. He was a very dark, big, tall, muscular, man with a kind, heavily lined face and graying hair. She guessed he was at least in his forties, and though she didn't think they were related, he treated Ford like his son. "What did Rice tell you was going on over at the Johnsons'?" she asked.

"He say there be some trouble over there, and Ford should hurry over to help Reverend Marsh. I should watch you and keep his rifle loaded and with me all the time," Morgan explained

"Come on up to the front of the store with me," she said, standing up wearily. "Nerva will be all right here for a little while." Morgan followed Harriet, and when they were far enough away where Nerva couldn't hear, Harriet told him what had happened to the Johnsons. "Thank you for being here with me Morgan. I think Reverend Marsh and Rice and Ford should be back soon."

Morgan was staring back at Nerva. "So that sweet girl got away," he said quietly. "She lucky to be alive, and now we'll take care of her."

"That's right Morgan. We'll do all we can for her, and hopefully she will be all right," Harriet said. "You go ahead and do what chores you need to. I'll stay with her and call you if she wakes up."

"I just gonna say somethin' to her first, Miz Marsh," he said, walking back to Nerva. Harriet watched as he knelt down and took Nerva's hand and whispered into her ear. So gentle, so loving, Harriet thought and she longed for Eli to come back.

*9*

A hot, mid-afternoon sun beat down on Eli and Rice and their parade of men, horses, wagon and coffins as they moved slowly down the road toward home. To escape the heat, they stopped in a shallow creek to cool off and let the horses drink. "Rice, we're going to have to get to work on another barn sooner than I thought," Eli said. "And finding lumber will be a problem with the armies blockading supplies."

Rice pulled the notice Harriet had given him out of his pocket. "Maybe we won't need another barn," he said, handing it to Eli. "Mother said some Union soldiers came by the Bee yesterday looking for you. They left that and hoped you might do some trading with them."

Eli stared at the notice. "They want to trade horses with me? I can't imagine why. If they were really desperate, they would just come in and take them."

Rice kicked the creek bank. "Maybe we should talk to them, now that we're going to have all these extra horses. What do you think they would want to trade back to us?"

"I have no idea," Eli said, leading Gray out of the creek. "But let's get going. I don't like it that your mother is there with only Morgan, especially with soldiers coming around."

In another hour, they crested the last hill. Below them lay the farm and the Bee across the road. They could see two horses tied to the rail outside the store. As they came down the hill, Morgan walked into the road to meet them. "Everything all right?" Eli called.

"Yassuh. We good," Morgan grinned. "But I sure happy to see all you."

"Who's here?" Rice asked, motioning to the other horses.

"That Mista Will Burkhart and Big Jim," Morgan answered. "They come to check on Miz Marsh."

"Rice, you all get these horses settled. Herm and I will get the Johnsons over to the church after I see your mother," Eli said, walking towards the Bee. But before he could get there, Harriet ran out the door and threw her arms around him and waved to Rice. Will and Big Jim followed her out the door.

"Thank goodness you're back," she cried, tears soaking her face and rolling down her dress.

"We're all right Harri," he whispered, hugging her and then shaking hands with Will and nodding to Big Jim.

"Terrible situation, Eli," Will said, shaking his head. I was worried about Harriet being here with just Morgan. So I brought Big Jim over to help out."

"Good of you Will. Since you're here, maybe you could help Herm and me get these coffins down to the church. We need to get them buried first thing tomorrow," Eli said.

Harriet walked to the back of the wagon. The sight of the two simple coffins side by side made her feel weak, and she leaned against the side for support. "It really happened like Rice said?" she asked.

Eli nodded. "Never seen anything like it, Harri. At least their suffering is over now."

"Did the sheriff have any ideas about who might have done

this?" Will asked.

"Not really," Eli answered. "They found a Confederate cap in the barn near some of the ropes like the ones that were used, but it might not mean anything. We're all hoping Nerva turns up and knows what happened."

Harriet grabbed his arm and pointed to the store. "She's here Eli. Morgan and I found her this morning in those bushes right over there!"

"What did she say?" he asked, hurrying into the store.

Harriet rushed after him. "Nothing. She's unconscious. We cleaned her up and we've been watching her all day, but she hasn't come to."

Kneeling down beside Nerva, Eli put his hand on her feverish forehead. He rubbed her wrists and patted her cheeks. "I've been doing that every hour," Harriet said. "I think we should let her rest, and then maybe she'll just wake up," she sniffed, feeling annoyed that everyone was so concerned about Nerva.

"We really need to talk to her, Eli," Will said. "Our whole community is on edge, worrying about who killed Mack and Mary. That girl surely knows something."

Eli stiffly got to his feet. "I feel the same way," he said. "But what if she doesn't know anything at all—then what? I agree with Harri. Let's see how she is tomorrow. We can put her in one of our extra rooms tonight in case she wakes up, can't we?" he asked, smiling at Harriet.

Harriet hadn't planned on that at all, but she didn't want to argue with Eli in front of Will. "I guess so," she answered quietly. "I'll go over and get a room ready while you're down at the church. Ford or Morgan can sit with Nerva."

Eli nodded toward to the coffins. "It won't take us long to get them settled for the night in the church," he said, walking out to the wagon with Will, where Herm was waiting. "We'll bury them tomorrow morning, and then I'll make Sunday's service their memorial."

"I'll check by tomorrow, Sis," Will said, hugging Harriet.

Big Jim brought the horses over from the water trough, and the three men mounted up and followed Herm's wagon down to the church. "Do you think you could help us out with some food when I get back?" Eli called back to Harriet. "Rice and Ford and I haven't eaten much in two days."

"I might be able to find something," she laughed and waved him away on her way back into the store to check on Nerva. Her condition was exactly the same, so Harriet left her and went across to the barn where Rice and Ford and Morgan were preparing stalls for the new horses.

"You all right Mother?" Rice called out when he saw her. "Morgan told us about Nerva. Is she awake yet?"

"No, she's not awake and yes, I'm fine," Harriet answered, trying not to sound annoyed. "I need one of you to sit with her a bit. Your father wants to move her up to the house for the night. So I'll have to get a room ready."

Rice peaked over the stall when he heard the tone of Harriet's voice. As hard as his mother tried to be open-minded about helping former slaves, she could not get past viewing them as lower class people. Offering one of them a room in her home would be out of the question. "It's probably just for one night, Mother," he said quietly, trying to make her feel better. "Ford can go down and sit with her now." He smiled and raised his eyebrows at Harriet. "It turns out they know each other pretty well."

"Good," she answered turning to leave, but she was not pleased at all with Rice's observation about Ford and Nerva. They certainly didn't need some low class romance going on right in their own home. Surely Eli didn't know this or he wouldn't have suggested taking Nerva in.

"Say Mother," Rice interrupted her thoughts. "We're all awfully hungry. Do you think we could eat early?"

"You all can eat when it's ready!" Harriet snapped and kept

walking toward the house. Making food—is that all they thought she did, she wondered. Didn't anyone care that she was dead tired from not sleeping, worrying, and working the horses and the store?

Rice watched his mother until she reached the house. He had never thought of her as being old, but she looked it today with her straggly hair, sagging shoulders, and heavy, slow feet. He wished he had not added to her angry mood, but he just couldn't understand her attitude sometimes. It was so different from his father's or even Uncle Will's and so closed off from the changes the War had already brought. What would happen to her when the War finally ended and their world was altered maybe again forever, he worried.

———

## 10

By the time Eli got home from the church, Harriet had worked through her mood. She had already had Ford carry Nerva to the house and put her to bed in the small corner room above the kitchen. Ford had seemed so worried that Harriet suggested that he sit with Nerva a while longer and keep talking to her. As Harriet rushed to fry chicken and boil potatoes and green beans, she could hear Ford's soft, deep voice urging Nerva to wake up and come back to him. His tenderness lifted her spirits and soothed her dark thoughts.

When Eli came in, he kissed her on the cheek and pointed up to the sound of Ford's voice in the room above. "That was very thoughtful of you, Harri."

Harriet shrugged. "You should get cleaned up before dinner. You smell worse than the outhouse," she laughed.

Eli laughed too and went to wash and change. Thank goodness Harri didn't know what she was really smelling. Handling human remains always left him with a lingering odor, but the Johnsons had been in such poor shape, he wondered if he would ever get the rotting

smell out of his nose and pores.

The slam of the front door and the sound of Rice's voice drifted up the stairs. "Smells great in here, Mother!"

"You get cleaned up too. You're almost as bad as your father," Harriet ordered. "And tell Ford to come down and take some plates of food out to the barn for Morgan and him tonight. I know they haven't had time to do anything about food."

Eli stepped out of his room when Rice got to the top of the stairs. "We need to make a plan tonight for moving the rest of the horses. Ask Morgan and Ford to come to the house after dinner," he said in a low voice.

Rice nodded his head. "Okay, Pop. I'll tell Ford now."

Harriet had all the food on the table when they came downstairs. Before they sat down, Eli said his usual blessing, but at the end, he gave thanks that they were all together and safe. He made a special plea for seeing them through the night and into another day. Subdued and exhausted, they ate in silence until Eli finally looked at Harriet and took her hand. "This is a wonderful dinner. I can't thank you enough for all you do for us."

Harriet smiled at him and then at Rice, ashamed that she had felt so angry earlier. "It's been a terrible couple of days for all of us, but now we're here together. That's all that really matters. I've got pie in the kitchen," she said, getting up.

"Rice and I are going to the porch to have a smoke and go over the next few days. I've asked Morgan and Ford to come over. You should join us too," Eli said.

"You two go ahead. I'll bring the pie out after I check on Nerva," she said, as she cleared the plates from the table.

Eli and Rice stood up and Rice patted his stomach. "Thanks for dinner Mother. I feel whole again." But to himself he thought— just like that—all the tension he felt from his mother in the barn was gone and she seemed happy. Thank God, Pop knows how to help her when she gets so dark.

———

*11*

Morgan and Ford sat quietly while Eli and Rice talked. "So early tomorrow Herm is going to dig the graves, and we'll get the Johnsons buried. Then we have to deal with our horses here and the horses that are still over at the other barn," Eli said.

"There's still about a dozen over there," Rice said. "If we could get Herm, and Uncle Will and Big Jim to help us, we could move them over in one trip."

"I still need one of you to stay here with Mrs. Marsh," Eli said looking at Morgan and Ford.

"Can I stay here this time, Reverend suh?" Ford asked.

"Yes, but you can't spend all your time with Nerva," Eli warned him. "We'll help with getting the horses out to pasture in the morning, but you will have to work all day getting everything ready for all these new ones coming over."

"Excuse me Reverend suh, but where we goin put them?" Morgan asked.

"Some will have to stay in the paddock at night until we

build more stalls," Rice said. "We can rotate them so the same ones aren't out every night. As long as it doesn't rain too much, we should be all right until fall."

Eli sighed and tapped his pipe on the railing. "Getting the lumber to enlarge the barn is going to be next to impossible. As long as the Confederates control the rail lines and roads out of Knoxville, nothing will get through."

Harriet walked out onto the porch carrying a tray of plates with pie. "How hard would it be to take apart the Johnson barn and bring it over here?" she asked, passing out the plates.

Eli thought for a minute. "Could be done," he answered. "But it would take a long time and too many trips back and forth. It's dangerous moving large loads on these roads now. If the bummers found out, they'd stop us for sure and take everything for the armies. I'm even worried about moving the horses tomorrow."

"Wouldn't we need permission from someone—I don't know who—to take down that barn?" Rice asked. "I mean Mack asked us to take his horses, but I don't think he meant the barn too!" he laughed.

"Don't you make fun of me, Rice," Harriet bristled. "I was just trying to think of where to get lumber quickly."

"I expect someone will take over that property soon enough, and they'll want that fine barn," Eli said. Sheriff Hawkins thinks our Governor Andrew Johnson was Mack's closest living relative. If that's true, he'll be the one to decide what happens over there."

Harriet laughed. "God help us if he moves here. He's just a poor tailor who got himself into politics. He knows nothing about farming or much of anything else in my opinion."

Not wanting Harriet to get started on politics, especially in front of Morgan and Ford, Eli said, "Having him as a neighbor isn't even worth thinking about. I doubt he'll ever come back here. We've got the War getting closer every day and now killers in our midst. Maybe the two are connected and maybe not, but we need to concentrate on being extra careful and vigilant."

Rice stood up and stretched. "So you're saying we may not be able to enlarge the barn by fall. That leaves us with way too many horses once it gets cold."

"I'll ask at the Sunday service if anyone is interested in stalling horses for us. But the truth is, no one else has a bigger barn than ours or the Johnsons'," Eli said.

"Let's talk to the Union army, Pop. They need horses, and we have plenty. Maybe it's a way we could help," Rice suggested.

Eli yawned and stood up slowly. "Maybe so, son, but right now I feel like a hundred years old and I need to sleep." He thanked Morgan and Ford for their help, and they left for the barn.

"I think I'll sit here a little longer," Rice said, as Harriet opened the porch door for Eli, and they climbed the stairs to their room. Harriet said nothing while she changed into her nightgown and brushed and braided her hair, but her heart was pounding. To herself she said over and over—Don't do it. Don't get involved in the War. Don't bring it into our home. Don't let it happen.

## 12

Eli was already asleep when Harriet got under the covers next to him. She tucked herself around him, and they slept spooning as they always did. Deep into the night, Eli thought he heard a cat crying outside, but then it became a shrieking sound so loud, he struggled to open his eyes and look around the room. Harriet was grabbing his arm and trying to pull him out of bed. "There's something in the house, Eli! Get up! Get up!" she hissed.

Shaking himself awake, Eli turned up the lamp by the bed and stood up. "Stay here," he whispered and opened the door.

Rice stepped into the hallway from his room at the same time. "What was that, Pop?"

Before Eli could answer, the screams started again. "It must be Nerva!" he said, rushing down the hallway with Rice behind him.

Inside the small room, Nerva was standing on the rug by the bed, screaming and then moaning and pointing towards the small closet. Her eyes darted back and forth and saliva foamed down her chin. Her dark, matted hair stood out sharply around her face.

When they tried to get near her, she punched and kicked at them.

"Get your Mother!" Eli shouted to Rice, but Harriet was already coming through the door.

Pushing Eli and Rice behind her, she put her arms around Nerva and spoke soothingly, saying over and over, "Sh… it's all right now. You're safe. No one's going to hurt you. Sh…Sh…Sh." Finally she was able to get Nerva to sit down on the bed. Harriet never stopped holding her, and then gradually she started rocking her back and forth until Nerva went limp in her arms, still whimpering off and on.

"Thank God," Eli said as Harriet motioned him and Rice to leave the room. In the hallway with the screaming stopped, they heard pounding on the front door and Morgan shouting, "Y'all right in there?"

Rice ran downstairs and opened the door. Morgan and Ford stood on the porch with rifles. "We're okay, no need for those," he said, pointing at the guns. "Nerva came to and started screaming."

"She awake now?" Ford asked, anxiously looking up the stairs.

"Not really," Rice said. "My mother is with her. She was able to calm her down, and now she seems to be asleep again."

"But she all right?" Ford asked.

"I think we'll know more tomorrow," Eli answered from the bottom of the stairs. "It's a good sign that she woke up, but you heard her. She's not normal yet."

"She's gone back to sleep," Harriet said, coming down the stairs and checking the clock in the hallway. "Mercy—it's nearly four o'clock. I might as well start some coffee. It'll be light soon."

"Did she say anything at all?" Eli asked.

"Nothing—just crying and moaning, poor thing," Harriet sighed, going into the kitchen.

Eli looked at Morgan and Ford. "Give her a little more time. She'll come around. You two go on back to the barn. We'll come over in a bit and get started. Thanks for rushing over here and watching out for us."

"Nothin goin happen here Reverend suh, if we can hep it," Morgan said.

Eli patted him on the shoulder. "I hope you're right."

———

## 13

June 4, 1863

Not looking forward to today. Have to bury Mack and Mary. Then go back for the rest of the horses. Finding Nerva here was a surprise. Wondering if she'll ever be able to tell us anything. Harri has been wonderful with her. Maybe she can coax her into talking. Rice wants me to take the Union army up on their offer to trade horses. What will that mean for us? If we make a deal, no one else must know. I'm thinking we could all be arrested by the Confederate army for helping the Union. And then there's Harri—she'll be furious with me if I get us involved in the War.

Herm was digging the second grave when Eli rode up to the church. Will and Big Jim were already there, standing by quietly. "I see y'all got going early too," Eli said, climbing off Gray.

"I'll be ready here in a few minutes, Reverend," Herm said, resting the shovel in a mound of red clay while he mopped the sweat off his face. "Did that girl ever wake up?"

Eli described Nerva's waking during the night. "That screaming scared us all to death," he said, shaking his head. "Harriet finally got her calmed down, but she never said anything."

Will who looked very much like Harriet, but had a reputation for being a hothead, shrugged his shoulders. "She does that again, and maybe somebody ought to give her a good shake. Sometimes that brings folks around you know."

Eli looked sharply at Will. "That seems too harsh to me. She's already scared out of her mind."

"Look Eli, here we are burying the Johnsons and we have no idea what happened to them. Everyone is worried they're gonna be next. And you and Harriet are treating Nerva like she's some kind of house guest!" Will said angrily.

Eli's face turned a dark red. The temptation to snap back at Will was overwhelming, but he looked down to collect himself and took a deep breath. "We're in a sacred place, and it's not a time to argue, Will. Let's do right by Mack and Mary." He turned away and walked toward the church with the other men following him. They brought the coffins out one by one and lowered them into the ground.

In the quiet of the morning, Eli recited the 23rd Psalm and the Lord's Prayer, before Herm and Big Jim filled the graves. "It's a relief to get them into the ground," he said, as they walked to their horses.

"I'm sorry I got angry back there," Will said.

"It's all right. I understand what you're thinking Will," Eli answered. "I'm more worried than you can imagine too, but we have to be patient. Look, Rice and I were wondering if you and Big Jim, and you too Herm, would be willing to help us get the rest of the horses this morning. Morgan's coming with us, but the more hands we have, the faster the move will go. It'll take most of the day, but then at least it will be done."

Herm and Will agreed and hurriedly rode home to tell their wives. Big Jim went back with Eli to help with the horses at the barn. They all agreed to meet at the Bee in two hours for the ride to the Johnsons'.

———

# 14

The ride back to the Johnsons' was quick, and they arrived easily before noon. Nothing appeared to have changed since Eli and Rice had left the day before. Again the horses were desperate to get out of the hot barn, and their rush to the paddock was wild and frenzied. After the air cleared in the barn, Will whispered to Eli, "Show me where."

Eli pointed, "Back there along the wall. You'll see the ropes."

Will went to look, but came back quickly, his face white. "Terrifying to think someone would do that to Mack and Mary," he managed to say.

Eli nodded. "Especially if it's someone we know. Let's get out of here. I hope I never have to come here again. Someone else will have to deal with that poor dead Black," he said, closing the barn doors.

Rice and Morgan were working at calming the horses with fresh water and feed, and they already had bridles and reins on some of the less agitated ones and the mules. A few were still running wildly and had to be chased down, but eventually all were secured and ready for the trip to their new home. Morgan and Big Jim each took three horses to trail behind them. Will and Herm each took two, while Eli took one and Rice took one and tied it to his saddle horn. Organized in this fashion, they rode down the drive and spread themselves out on the road.

They kept a slow pace to keep the horses as calm as possible, and before long both men and horses were sweating heavily in the intense afternoon sun. "Let's stop in the creek up ahead and cool off a bit," Eli shouted. Soon they were relaxing in the dense shade and cooling waters of the wide creek.

"Where y'all headin?" a high pitched voice called out of the bushes on the far side of the creek.

Eli raised one hand in his Be Quiet and Wait motion that Rice recognized from his childhood. No one else in the group moved or answered.

"I guess mebbe they didn't hear ya," another voice called from a little farther upstream on the other side.

Two Confederate soldiers stepped out on different sides of the creek, pointing rifles at the group. "We don't mean ya no harm," the first one who had spoken said. In the dark shade, he appeared to be the older of the two, but they were so filthy and disheveled looking, it was hard to tell much about either one.

"What do you want?" Will finally asked.

"Y'all got any food?" the younger one asked.

"I've got a jam sandwich you can have," Herm said, reaching into his saddle bag. Then he climbed off his horse and waded through the creek to hand it to him.

Eli was thinking that today was one of the first times he could remember that Harri hadn't given him some biscuits before he left. "I'm sorry. We don't seem to have much to offer you," he said. "We're just moving these horses to a new barn, so we didn't bring food."

"Save me some of that sandwich, Jay," the older one shouted

across the creek.

"Where's the rest of your detail?" Will asked.

"They're not far. We're sorta like scouts," the older one answered, still pointing his gun at them.

"Yeah, scouts," laughed the one called Jay.

"Look men, if there's nothing else we can help you with, we need to get back on the road," Eli said. It seemed to him that despite the guns, they were probably not in danger from these soldiers who appeared to be starving runaways.

"Y'all got far to go?" the older one asked. "Cause ya know, we could mebbe hep ya," he offered.

"Not too far," Eli answered, not wanting to say exactly where. "Thank you, but we'll be fine. Would you mind lowering your guns?"

"What do ya think Jay? Shouldn't we hep 'em out with a couple of those horses?" the older one asked, keeping his gun raised.

"Let's hep these slave boys with theirs," Jay laughed.

"Good idea," the older one answered, motioning towards Morgan and Big Jim to move away from their horses.

Jay sloshed through the creek and took the reins for both Morgan and Big Jim's saddled horses, and then walked them over to the other bank alongside the older soldier.

"So you need to borrow our horses for awhile," Eli said in a quiet voice. "We're happy to lend them to you, aren't we?" he said, opening his arms to the group. Rice, Will and Herm all nodded in agreement, while Morgan and Big Jim looked down and stayed quiet.

"Borrow, sure that's right. And when we don't need 'em no more, we'll bring 'em back. Mighty nice of ya to let us hep ya out this way," the older one laughed, as they mounted the horses.

"Yeah, we'll be seein ya," Jay snickered, as they rode away waving and laughing.

Eli and the others stayed in the creek, watching them until they were out of sight. Will exhaled loudly, "At least they're not going the same way we are. You think they're runaways?"

Eli frowned. "Most likely, don't be so sure that they won't circle around and follow us, so they can 'hep us' some more. Let's get home as fast as we can."

Rice turned to Morgan and Big Jim. "You two okay with bareback?"

"Yes suh, Mr. Rice. It the natural way," Morgan said smiling, and he and Big Jim heaved themselves onto two of the horses they had been trailing. The rest of the group hurriedly got mounted and they rode off towards the Marsh farm. To their great relief, they saw no more of the two soldiers. The farm and the Bee looked quiet when they crested the hill.

———

# 15

Ford met them in the road in front of the Bee. He was carrying one of Rice's rifles. "Anything happen?" Eli asked, dismounting.

"Group of Union soldiers rode through earlier, Reverend suh, but they didn stop," Ford answered, just as Harriet walked out of the store waving to everyone.

"How's Nerva, Mother?" Rice asked.

"She's better. She's sitting up in there," Harriet said pointing back to the store. "And before you ask, she hasn't said a word yet."

"Have you asked her what happened?" Will asked, moving closer to his sister.

"No. I asked her how she felt and she just stared ahead like she didn't see or hear me," Harriet answered. "I can't make her talk, but at least she's not screaming her head off."

"She don seem to know me neither," Ford said sadly.

"Rice, you need to move these horses up to the paddock, so Herm and Will and Big Jim can get on home. And fix Big Jim up with a fresh horse and saddle—Will, your choice. I'll be up there directly," Eli said, putting his arm around Harriet and trying to get the talk away from Nerva's condition.

"Why were Morgan and Big Jim riding bareback?" Harriet asked, staring into Eli's face as they walked into the store.

Eli exhaled and took off his hat and rubbed his face. "Two Confederate soldiers surprised us while we were cooling off back up the road in the creek. First they asked for food and then they took two horses and laughed about it."

Harriet's face turned white. "Did they hurt you?" she asked anxiously.

"No, everyone is fine, but they held rifles on us the whole time. So we agreed to giving them the horses. Then they rode off towards Jonesborough—not here—thank the Lord," he said, sitting down heavily and looking over at Nerva.

Harriet looked at Nerva too. "Could they be the ones?" she asked.

"Anything is possible, Harri," he sighed. "But these two seemed too down and out to do anything like that. Anyway, from the look of things over at the Johnsons', it was more than two people who killed them."

As Eli said these words, Nerva began to sob and rock back and forth. Harriet sat down beside her and put her arm around her. "You're safe here," she said quietly, rubbing her arm.

"So I guess she understood what we were talking about," Eli said, marveling at Harriet's attitude towards Nerva. "It won't be long before she's talking, thanks to you Harri," he added, getting up and walking toward the door. "I'm going to see how Rice is organizing the horses up at the barn and say good-bye to Will and Herm. Then I've got to start working on my sermon for Sunday. I'll be at the house if you need me."

"I'm going to close up here pretty soon. We can have dinner early tonight. We need a good night's sleep after last night," Harriet sighed. "Maybe Nerva will allow it," she added, frowning at the girl.

Eli didn't answer and when Harriet looked up, he was already crossing the road toward the barn. His shoulders were sagging and his boots were dragging his feet along. He seemed to have aged ten years over the last few days.

After dinner, Eli closed the doors to his library and took out the sermon he had started earlier. But after staring at the pages for several minutes, he pulled out his diary instead.

*June 4, 1863 continued*

*I was wrong this morning when I wrote about not looking forward to today because of having to bury Mack and Mary and moving the rest of the horses. The worst part was being held at gunpoint by those rogue soldiers. My weakness for horses put all our lives at risk. We could have been killed. Worried they may have followed us and know where we live. Must keep standing watch day and night. How can I find the strength to preach about the understanding of God's mysterious ways when I 'm so afraid and unconvinced myself? The Devil is bearing down on us.*

Harriet and Rice were sitting on the side porch when they heard the riders coming up the road. The rose bushes and wisteria vines shielded them from view, but they could clearly see six Union soldiers pausing at the end of the drive to the house. One was pointing towards the Bee and then directly at the house.

"Mother, quick get Pop," Rice whispered. Harriet nodded and moved quietly down the side porch and around to the back door and slipped in.

Lost in his thoughts about the way the Devil worked, Eli jumped when Harriet opened the door and put her fingers to her lips. "Union soldiers are coming up our drive," she whispered.

Eli closed his diary, and with Harriet right behind, hurried to the front door, just in time to see two officers dismounting. The others, all enlisted men, remained on their horses. Rice came around to the front porch just as Eli stepped out and greeted them, "Good evening gentlemen. What can we do for you?"

One of the officers removed his hat. "Good evening sir. Sorry to disturb all of you this late. Are you Eli Marsh?"

Eli nodded. "How can I help you, sir?"

"I'm Major William Carrigan and this is Lieutenant John Hunt," he said, extending his hand to Eli. "We'd like to talk to you about your horses."

Eli smiled. "This is my wife Harriet and my son Rice. I'm always happy to talk about horses. Why don't we sit down," he said, motioning to the rocking chairs.

"Can we offer you some cool water from our springhouse, Major Carrigan?" Harriet asked.

"That's very kind of you, but we don't have much time," the Major answered, easing down into one of the rockers. "This is a wonderfully private porch," he added, looking around. "The War feels far away here doesn't it," he sighed, shaking his head.

"Yes, most of the time," Eli agreed. "But there are hardly any families around here who haven't lost someone or something because of it."

The Major cleared his throat. "Yes, I know that all too well," he said. "Still it's comforting to find a safe place like this once in a while, and I thank you for that. Look Reverend, we've heard that you and most of your neighbors are still loyal to our country and Mr. Lincoln, even though your state has joined the Confederacy. It feels like that might be true, at least for you folks, judging from our welcome here tonight," he said, looking steadily at Eli and leaning forward in his chair.

"That's true enough," Eli answered. "But I try to stay as neutral as possible in order to better serve my small congregations. Their sentiments fall on both sides for good reasons. It's not my place to judge them."

"But you personally are a friend to the Union, is that right?" the Major asked.

Eli pulled out his pipe and tobacco pouch and was nodding his head in agreement when the wailing sound came from the upstairs. Everyone flinched, and Harriet jumped up and said, "Oh that girl— there she goes again!" and hurried inside.

The Major frowned. "Is someone else here?" he asked.

"We have a young woman staying with us for a while. She's recovering from a terrible shock and wakes up crying sometimes," Eli answered. He watched the Major carefully to see if the explanation meant anything to him, but his face showed nothing. "So Major, you wanted to talk about our horses?" he asked.

"That's right. We heard that you keep a fine herd of horses here. I don't know if you know it or not, but our army is always in need of fresh horses and mules and especially now in this area. We were hoping we might be able to strike up a partnership with you," he finished, pulling a cigar out of his pocket.

Silence filled the porch. Eli and Rice stared at each other, while the Major and the Lieutenant stared at them. Finally the Major broke the quiet. "Will Mrs. Marsh mind if I smoke this?" he asked, holding up the cigar.

"As long as we're outside, it's all right," Eli chuckled. "That one probably smells a lot better than those rolled up tobacco leaves Rice likes to smoke."

"Here, try one of these," the Major said, handing one to Rice.

Rice took the cigar and sniffed the sweetness of the fine cured tobacco. "Thank you, Major. It's been a while since I've had one of these. Say, are you the one who left that notice with my mother a few days ago?"

"That was one of my men. We've been posting them around here when we thought it was safe," he said.

"Sorry to interrupt, sir," Lieutenant Hunt said. "But it's getting pretty dark."

Major Carrigan stood up. "Yes, we need to get back. Mind if we come around tomorrow to take a look at your horses?" he asked, turning to Eli.

"I'll be here in the afternoon, and of course you're welcome to stop by, but you haven't really told me what kind of partnership you're talking about," Eli pointed out.

"We can talk more about it tomorrow," the Major said, hurrying to join the rest of the soldiers, as they rode off into the darkness.

Rice whistled softly. "A partnership with the Union—what do you think, Pop?"

Eli shook his head. "Strange, I guess we'll find out tomorrow. But whatever it is, you'll be in the thick of it, managing the horses."

"How dangerous is this going to be?" Harriet asked, staring at them from the porch door.

"Everything is dangerous around here, Mother," Rice answered. "But that doesn't mean we shouldn't help if we can."

"Rice is right," Eli agreed. "Something's about to happen here. Maybe it's true  they're going to try to secure control of Knoxville and drive the Confederates away like Sheriff Hawkins said. That would be a reason they'd be looking for more horses."

Sadness and dread made Harriet tremble. "They're going to bring this War right into our house," she murmured.

"And then we'll be just like everyone else," Rice said, leaving the porch and walking toward the paddock.

———

## 16

Nerva was quiet through the rest of the night, and with Morgan stationed on the front porch, all the Marshes slept soundly. Eli and Rice got up at dawn and went to the barn with Morgan. Ford had already started to turn the horses out to graze. As the last ones raced into the field, Major Carrigan and Lieutenant Hunt and the four soldiers rode up to the paddock. The sky was overcast and the air was heavy with rain, making it difficult to tell exactly what time it was, but Eli knew it was still very early and he was surprised to see them. He was certain they must be camping very close by—maybe in the woods up the road—and that worried him.

"Good morning gentlemen," he greeted them as they dismounted.

The soldiers stared at the array of beautiful Tennessee Walkers, American Saddlebreds, Morgans, and Chestnuts grazing in the field behind the paddock. "I can't believe what I'm seeing!" the Major exclaimed. "We had no idea you had so many and such a variety," he said looking at Eli. "Your reputation as a horseman is greatly underrated, Reverend. How many do you have?"

Embarrassed by the compliment, Eli shook his head. "You've come at an unusual time, Major Carrigan. We normally keep around twenty-five or thirty at the most here. But we've just taken in twenty more, plus a few mules, from a neighbor who passed away. You're looking at about fifty animals in all," he said, again studying the Major's face for any recognition of the Johnson murders.

"Are those Arabians out there in the far pasture?" the Major asked, squinting his eyes and ignoring the information about the neighbor.

"Yes, they're beauties aren't they—very spunky and durable too," Eli said smiling. "We've just started trying to breed them. Rice thinks they're the horses of the future."

While Eli and the Major were talking, Rice and Lieutenant Hunt walked out into the field for a closer look. "These are fine looking horses, Reverend Marsh," the Lieutenant said excitedly when they came back. "Rice tells me you don't have room for all of them in your barn."

"That's true enough," Eli sighed. "We're hoping to enlarge the barn soon, but we're in kind of a bind because we can't get any lumber or supplies right now.

A light rain started to fall and Eli suggested they move into the barn until the shower passed. Inside, the men seated themselves on bales of hay and overturned crates. Morgan and Ford were cleaning the stalls, and Eli motioned to them to join the group. The Major pulled out his cigars, but Eli put his hand up. "Sorry, no smoking in here—too much danger of fire," he said.

"Very wise," the Major said. "Look Reverend Marsh, we'd like to propose a partnership with you and Rice."

"Yes, you mentioned that last night. What exactly do you mean?" Eli asked, cocking his head.

"We have two needs. We must quickly add to our supply of horses in this area. It's too risky and time consuming for us to attempt to move more down from up North. So we'd like to buy some of your horses right away. At the same time, some of the horses we have are not fit enough for battle. They're tired and need rehabilitation. We are hoping we can stable them with you for a month or so, and you and Rice can bring them along and help them regain their strength.

Eli stroked his beard. "That's an interesting proposition, Major. What were you thinking of offering for our horses?"

"We can offer you $150 a horse, plus you'll be getting our horses in trade. Any that we can't take back become yours," the Major said.

Eli looked at Rice. "Mind if I talk this over with my son and our hands?" he asked.

The Major stood up. "It's stopped raining. We'll wait outside."

When the soldiers were out of earshot, Eli said in a low voice, "I think I'm willing to do this, but we'll all be at risk. It's likely a partnership like this will be considered traitorous if the Confederates find out. I need to know how you feel."

"On the other hand, this could be a good deal for us, Pop, if we can limit the number of horses they can bring here to rehabilitate," Rice whispered. "What do you two think? he asked, turning to Morgan and Ford.

"Dangerous fo sure," Morgan said. "But Ford here and I worry most evry day that somethin bad could happn. We be thankful to have a home and jobs at all. Ain't that right Ford?"

Ford looked at Eli and Rice. "Y' all been good to us Reverend Marsh. We gonna do whatever yous want."

"All right then, let's tell them," Eli said, walking ahead of the others out the barn door to where the soldiers were gathered. "I think we have a deal Major," he said, smiling and extending his hand.

Major Carrigan shook Eli's hand and then Rice's. "This will be an enormous help to our army, Reverend, and it won't be forgotten. I'd like to start making the trades as soon as possible."

"I understand, but first I have two conditions which you may not like," Eli said.

The Major frowned. "What do you mean?"

"We can't take any diseased horses. I hear that glanders is

widespread among the horses in both armies. If that got started in our barn, we'd be finished," he said, remembering years before watching horses suffer horrible deaths from the disease. It quickly spread through their bodies, erupting in infectious sores on their skins and then inside their noses, throats and lungs. Spreading like fire, it killed whole herds in a few days.

"I completely agree with you on that one," the Major said. "But we haven't seen any glanders here so far. Farther up north and out in Vicksburg, they've had a hell of a time. What's the other thing you want, Reverend?"

Eli stroked his beard. "Our personal horses and the Arabians will not be part of any trades."

"So you want to separate out certain horses that won't be available to us. Is that right?" the Major asked, scowling.

Eli nodded. "You're still going to have plenty to choose from Major."

"You sure we can't persuade you to part with those Arabians?" Lieutenant Hunt asked, clearly disappointed. "They're supposed to have amazing stamina and be very courageous in a fight."

"I wouldn't know about that, but we're just getting started with them and they're not for sale yet," Eli answered, looking at Rice for support.

Rice nodded his head in agreement. "I bought two at an auction in Greeneville three years ago. No one knew much about them around here, but I liked what I saw. So far the mare has produced a foal each year, but we still think of them as new to our farm and we'd like to build them up."

"I think we can honor your requests, Reverend. Let's see how things work out. Is there anything else we should know about?" the Major asked.

Before Eli could answer, Rice said, "You see how crowded we are sir. How many horses might you be bringing us to nurse along?"

"It'll have to be a gradual transfer," the Major answered.

"We don't want to raise folks' suspicions by riding around with a large number of horses and risk being followed here. We'll try our best not to overwhelm you with more than you can handle. And just maybe we can free up some lumber your way, so you can get started on your barn. My one condition is that none of you tell anyone else about our partnership. Is that understood?" he finished, staring intently at them.

"And you won't be telling anyone else about what's happening here either, Major, right?" Eli asked.

"No one else will know. I give you my word," the Major answered, extending his hand to Eli and then to Rice.

"And we give you ours," Eli replied, sealing the partnership.

"We'll stop by to pick up a few horses in the next few days," the Major said, as he and the other soldiers mounted up.

Eli asked that they not come the next day because it was Sunday and he never did business other than the Lord's on that day. The Major answered with a nod and a wave, as the soldiers rode away. Eli, Rice, Morgan and Ford all stared after them and then at each other, wondering where this secret arrangement would take them.

"Let's get some breakfast and tell your mother," Eli said, turning to Rice.

"I think I'll just eat up here at the barn," Rice laughed, looking at Morgan and Ford. "I like a peaceful breakfast, and Mother won't be serving that when she hears about this."

"Coward!" Eli laughed too. "I thought I heard you knew so much about how to handle the ladies."

Rice's face turned beet red, but before he could think of what to say, Eli had walked away toward the house, still laughing to himself. Rice watched him from behind, wondering what his comment about the ladies meant. His father rarely mentioned women other than his mother around him. What would it be like to talk to him about their mysteries and comforts? Had Eli ever enjoyed other women besides his mother and if so, who were they and where were they now? Impossible to imagine, and he doubted that he would ever know, but he felt sweaty all over just thinking about it. Thankfully Morgan and Ford had gone to their quarters to make breakfast and couldn't see him painfully leaning against the fence and trying to get control of himself. "God Lelia, I need you now," he whispered, and wondered if he could get away to see her that evening or maybe tomorrow after church. A sweet, beautiful vision of Lelia, with her soft, creamy skin and thick, dark hair sweeping over her shoulders when she untied it, crowded his brain. Lying down with Lelia felt like flying through the stars in the safety of her arms and legs wrapping him tightly. "Gotta stop thinking about this," he muttered, as he forced himself to walk out into the pasture. Watching the horses graze always calmed him down and soon his craving for Lelia began to ebb. He felt let down and now sad looking at these beautiful, majestic animals. Soon they would be harnessed into military training, working their hearts out or worse being slaughtered by hailing bullets— all to serve their new masters in the name of country.

"C'mon in Mr. Rice," Morgan called. "We got you some bacon and eggs goin'."

"I'll be right there!" Rice shouted, wondering how long Morgan had been watching him.

———

## 17

Harriet's reaction to the details of the new partnership was just as Rice predicted. "There will be nothing but trouble, if you do this," she said, scowling at Eli. "How do you know you can trust these soldiers? What if someone finds out and tells the Confederates?"

Eli pursed his lips and looked down at his breakfast plate. "I know, Harri. It's risky business, but I trust Major Carrigan's word, just as I believe he trusts mine. Besides, we've seen fewer Confederate troops around here than Union ones lately. I truly believe they're gearing up to make a run on Knoxville, probably in the fall."

"So this partnership is only for a couple of months?" Harriet asked, feeling a little relieved.

"I'm thinking so, Harri," he said, putting his arms around her. "Rice and I want to make this work, but it's no good if you won't support us. We need you," he whispered into her ear.

Harriet sighed, knowing Eli was determined to go ahead with the trading. "All right," she murmured. "But if something bad happens, I won't forgive you for bringing trouble into our home," she said, turning away and wiping her eyes.

Eli sat down at the table and started picking at his eggs. Trying to think of something else to talk about, he asked, "How's Nerva?"

"Oh, she's talking a bit," Harriet answered, without turning around.

"What? Why didn't you tell me?" he cried, jumping out of his chair.

"Well, it just happened this morning, and you weren't here," Harriet said calmly. "Anyway, all she said was 'Yes'm' when I asked her if she wanted some tea and a biscuit."

"Well, at least that's something," Eli sighed, sitting back down. "I'll go up and see her directly."

Upstairs, the little bedroom over the kitchen was already hot and stuffy, but Eli found Nerva tightly bundled up in a quilt, shivering. She didn't look up when he spoke to her, nor did she seem to hear any of his questions. Finally he gave up and walked into the hallway. Turning back to look at her, he said, "I wish you'd talk to us Nerva, because if you don't, I'm afraid Sheriff Hawkins will decide to take you over to Greeneville. He'll put you up somewhere, and I'm sure it won't be very comfortable. We can help you here and maybe find work for you, but you have to start talking to us."

Eli's words caused Nerva to raise her head and stare up at him, but when she said nothing, he turned and walked away. He hoped she would take his words seriously, because he was positive that Hawkins would be coming back soon, sniffing around. He'd most likely take Nerva into some sort of protective custody, and they would never see her again. He wondered if Nerva had any free papers at all, or if the Johnsons were harboring her as a runaway, and she just stayed on. Ford probably knows, but he might not say, he thought, as he reached the door to his library. Maybe Ford should marry Nerva—that would at least give her the protection of a husband who's a free man. I'll talk to Harri about this, he decided, as he closed the door and pulled out his diary.

Saturday, June 5, 1863

It's done. Rice and I are in partnership with the Union to trade horses with them and see if we can save some of their failing ones. Treacherous business for all. Harri is certain I'm bringing danger and evil into our home. Rice and I see this as a chance to help our country, but we may end up paying a heavy price. Those two Confederate soldiers who stole our horses at the creek know we have a lot more. What if they tell their officers and then they come to us wanting horses too? We'll be caught in the middle or worse.

I've got this idea about Nerva. If I could convince Ford to marry her, we could most likely keep her here. Someday maybe she'll tell us who killed the Johnsons. God forgive me, I've sunk into manipulating both horses and humans now.

———

18

The Sunday service was overflowing with worshipers, some that Eli hadn't seen near the church in many years. Late comers stood two and three deep at the back or leaned against the side walls. Eli stuck to his notes and gave a short eulogy, talking about Mack and Mary's many contributions to the Limestone community and the many people whose lives were saved and improved because of them. After the last hymn and benediction, he asked everyone to stop by their graves and offer their personal prayers.

As people were standing to leave the sanctuary, Jacob Thompson blocked the church doors. "Excuse me Reverend Marsh, but myself and a lot of others here need to hear from you what exactly happened over at the Johnsons' place. There are a lot of rumors going around," he said. Other voices clamored "Yes" and "Please."

Eli spread his arms wide and looked at Rice and Harriet. "I'll tell you what I know for anyone who wants to stay, but I think mothers should take children outside." Most of the crowd sat back down and waited for the children to be taken out. Eli stood by the pew where Rice and Harriet sat. In a quiet voice, he described what he and Rice had found at the Johnsons'. Some of the women wiped their eyes or held handkerchiefs over their mouths. The men looked at each other angrily. "Nerva is still with us. She's just starting to talk. So maybe we'll learn something from her soon," Eli finished.

For a few minutes no one said anything, and then it seemed that everyone started talking at once. "So what are we supposed to do Reverend?" Thompson shouted out over the noise. "Just wait for them to attack someone else?"

Eli raised his hands and asked for quiet. "We don't know who 'they' are yet, Jacob, and as far as I know, nothing else unusual has happened. Sheriff Hawkins will be back over here soon. Maybe he'll know something," he said. "Right now we should be watching out for ourselves and each other, and spread the word if we see or hear anything."

The din of people talking about protecting themselves grew louder until William Taylor, one of the old abolitionists, stood up. "I believe the Confederates or their sympathizers killed Mack and Mary. Most of us have known for years, they've been actively helping folks heading North to freedom. Lately, especially since Harold and Jimmy were killed, Mack's been going around saying terrible, evil things about the Confederacy. He absolutely could not tolerate his boys being drafted into their army and then he lost them forever. Someone around here decided to put an end to it."

The deafening talk erupted as soon as Taylor finished. Eli put his hands up and raised his voice, asking the crowd to calm down. "Good friends, we have no proof of anything yet. Like I said before, we all need to keep our eyes and ears open and let each other know if something else happens. Otherwise, I think it's best that we all go on home and go about our lives as much as possible," he urged.

Harriet and Rice stood up and walked with Eli to the door. The congregation followed them, and they stopped outside and greeted each family. William Taylor leaned toward Eli's ear as they shook hands. "I'm certain I'm right about this Reverend. It's the

Confederate sympathizers we should be watching out for," he whispered loudly.

"Thanks for speaking up, William. You may be right," Eli answered grimly. "It's hard to believe that people we count as friends and neighbors could do something like that, but we must consider it now."

Even as Eli said good-bye to the last of the crowd and he and Harriet and Rice were pulling away from the church, quite a few couples were still talking in the cemetery near the Johnson graves. "Maybe I should go back," Eli worried.

"Absolutely not," Harriet said. "You've done all you can. People have to look out for themselves and decide what to do."

———

# 19

As soon as Sunday lunch was over, Rice rushed off to call on Lelia. He had barely had a chance to talk to her after church, except to ask if he could come by that afternoon. Everyone knew that the Pattons sided with the Confederacy. So the opinions voiced so loudly at the church clearly made them feel uncomfortable, and they hurried away as quickly as they could. Rice wondered if Lelia would turn away from him now under her parents' pressure.

Riding up the long, shaded drive to the big columned plantation style house, Rice could see Lelia waiting on the front porch. She ran down the steps to meet him when he got near the house. Dressed in riding pants with a white, gauzy shirt and wide brimmed hat, she smiled up at him. "I've put up a basket for us. I thought we could take a ride," she said, taking his hand.

Rice smiled. "Perfect. It's a beautiful afternoon."

"But before we go, Daddy wants to talk to you," she said, putting her hand on his good arm. "He's waiting in the side garden where it's cool."

"What's this about?" Rice asked frowning.

"I'm not sure, but I think it's probably about what happened at church today. Hurry and talk to him, so we can get going," she said, pushing him toward the garden.

Rice went around the side of the house. Tall pine trees, coupled with large pink crepe myrtles and white hydrangeas and ferns lined the path to the shady side garden. The smell of cigar smoke met him long before he walked into the garden. "Hello, Rice," John Patton called from a large wicker rocker in the corner.

"Good afternoon, sir—Lelia said you wanted a word," Rice said, removing his hat and extending his hand to this heavy-set man with a wide, sweat-shiny face and balding gray hair. Still dressed in his white Sunday suit and string tie, Patton gripped Rice's hand tightly.

"Haven't seen you lately. Sit down," he said, motioning to another rocker.

Rice settled into the plush, pillowed chair and rocked back a bit. "I know, sir. I'm sorry about that. Pop's horses and the farm have been keeping me too busy. I guess you know we took in the Johnson horses. That's a bit of a burden right now."

"Damnable business at the Johnsons'. What did you and your father think of that rabble after church today?" he asked.

"We're very worried, sir, but don't you think all that talk just goes along with what's happening around here? I mean families and friends are taking sides against each other and saying all sorts of nasty things about the North and the South. Pop is trying to stay neutral, so he can help everyone, but it's hard," Rice said, looking away. He wondered what Mr. Patton would say if he knew about the partnership he and Eli had just formed with the Union. He was certain he would view it as a shameful betrayal , when really it was just sensible business for the Marshes.

"Humph," Patton grunted. "I understand your father's situation, but mark my words, you all won't be able to stay neutral forever. This is a Confederate state, and things are changing. Being friendly with the Union won't be an option much longer even in East Tennessee. You'll share my advice with your father won't you, Rice?"

"Yes sir," Rice answered, standing up. "You'll excuse me sir, if there's nothing else, Lelia wants to go for a ride."

Patton stood up smiling. "She can be impatient, I know. Y'all have a good time and don't stay away so long," he said, patting Rice on the back.

Rice was halfway up the path leading out of the garden, when Patton caught up with him. "One more thing son," he said. "Don't stray off our property this afternoon. Too many loose guns roaming around, you know?"

"Yes sir," Rice nodded. "We'll stay close," he said, thankful to be getting away from this oppressive man. Sweet Jesus, he thought to himself. Lelia and I will be history if Mr. Patton finds out what Pop and I are doing. Maybe I should just go ahead and ask her to marry me now before it's too late.

Lelia was waiting with the horses. She searched his face when he got close. "Everything all right with Daddy?"

"Seems to be, he wants us to stay close on your land," he answered, helping her climb onto her horse. So they decided to ride to the creek in the nearby woods that bordered the Patton property. There the water formed a series of shallow pools, deep enough to wade or even submerge into the cascading coolness. Big broad boulders offered places to sit and picnic or to just lie back and catch the sun sifting through the canopy of trees.

They didn't talk much during the ride, just enjoyed being together, galloping across the fields. Leaving the horses to graze in the thick grass lining the creek, they collected the food basket and blankets, took off their boots and waded through the water to one of the tabletop boulders. Sitting side by side, dangling their feet in the rushing water, Lelia rubbed Rice's leg. "You're so quiet today. What's wrong?" she asked.

"Nothing's wrong, really," he said, putting his arm around

her. "It's just these past few days—I've never seen anything like it. You can't imagine the horror over at the Johnsons', and now Nerva is staying at my parents' house and screaming half the time. I tell you the first time she did that, it gave me the shakes. I think she knows what happened over there and is scared out of her mind."

"How can I help?" she asked, moving her hand to his inner thigh.

"Honey, just being with you makes me feel better," he said taking her hand to stop the massaging, before it became irresistible. "And what you're thinking about right now would be fine, but I think we should talk first."

"All right," Lelia sighed and lay back on the rock. "What should we talk about?"

"Let's talk about us," he said. "'Cause everything else that's going on is too damn depressing."

Lelia was looking at his strong back and his dark hair curling over his collar. She wished he'd take off his shirt, so she could rub his back. But because of his withered arm, he rarely removed his shirt even when they were making love. "What about us, Rice?" she asked quietly.

Rice turned and looked at her. She was so beautiful lying on the blanket with her hair spread out around her flushed face. He was always happy with her and he knew he would be miserable and lonely if her father separated them because of his family's ties to the Union. His throat ached and he couldn't get his breath, but he managed to blurt out, "Lelia, let's get married." Except for the sound of the rushing waters, the world around them stopped, and the words floated in the air above. Lelia stared back at him as tears slid down her cheeks.

"I thought you would never ask me," she finally said, laughing softly and stretching out her arms to him and hugging him tightly.

"You're sure?" Rice asked, pulling back and stroking her hair. "'Cause you know, I'm not exactly perfect."

"You are to me," she said simply, making him smile, and

this time when they kissed, it felt different. It was the beginning of the two of them running forward through a world gone crazy, rising above all the fighting and killing and the misery of mourning the dead. "You'll have to ask Daddy," she murmured. "Of course he'll say yes, but you still have to ask him."

Rice took a deep breath. "I'll talk to him, but I don't have much of my own to offer as a husband yet. I mean we'll have to live with my folks for a while until we can build a place of our own. We won't have much time to ourselves. What will you do all day while I'm gone working the horses and the farm?"

"Rice, I've loved you all my life, even when you were going around with all those other girls. I can be patient for a little while until we get our own place," she said quietly.

"I just don't want you to be unhappy and feel trapped at home with my mother. She can be hard sometimes," he said, frowning.

"I can get along, and maybe she'll surprise you and even like having me around!" Lelia laughed. "You're not trying to talk me out of marrying you, are you?"

Rice pulled her close again. "Never—you're mine now. I'll talk to my folks tonight and then I'll ride back over here as soon as I can and ask your father. Let's start back," he said, sliding off the boulder and reaching up to help her down. "Just so you know, Lelia, you've always been the one. Those other girls were just for funning around," he laughed.

"That's very comforting to know, Rice, but it'll just be me and you funning around forever now," she giggled, splashing creek water on him with her foot.

Hand and hand they waded back to where they had left the horses, but they were no where to be seen on the creek bank. "They're probably out in the field. Wait here in the shade while I look for them," Rice said, pulling on his boots. Then shielding his eyes from the late afternoon sun, he walked out across the field.

Waiting in the coolness, Lelia excitedly began thinking

about their wedding, where it would be and what her dress would look like. She couldn't wait to talk to her mother about all the details. Lost in the happiness of becoming Rice's wife, she heard no sound behind her when a heavy arm clamped around her chest at the same time a handkerchief filled with dirt was shoved over her nose and down her mouth. She tried to push loose and scream, but the dirt and thick cloth clogged her throat, choking off her breath. A heavy body pushed her face down on the bank and tied her hands behind her back. Grass and mud swam in front of her eyes as she felt her blouse and pants being ripped away and her legs being spread wide. Dimly she could see dark sleeved arms bracing beside her head on the bank. "See how you like being married to that one-arm Southern boy after this," a raspy voice grunted into her ear just before the pain ripped into her from behind, and her world, now changed forever, went black.

———

# 20

Rice's first thought when he started to come to was, what's that in my ear, and his second was, why couldn't he open his eyes? He tried to lift his head, but a searing pain shot through him making it too painful to move. He forced his eyes open and stared up at the darkening sky. Horse's legs were next to him, and he recognized Sassy's nose nuzzling his cheek. It must have been her nibbling his ear that brought him around. Finally he was able to sit up enough to look around. He felt the blood and dirt clumped on the back of his head, and some was still trickling down his neck, soaking his shirt. "Where the hell am I?" he asked hoarsely. Barely able to turn his head, he glimpsed Lelia's horse, Mustard, munching grass closer to the woods. "Lelia, where are you?" he called out weakly. He was trying to crawl over to Mustard when he heard riders coming. Laying back down, he looked up to see John Patton and two of his farmhands riding up.

"WHERE'S LELIA?" Patton shouted, jumping off his horse.

"I don't know," Rice mumbled, trying to sit up again.

"WE'VE GOT TO FIND HER. LOOK AROUND!" Patton yelled to his men.

Patton knelt down beside Rice and gave him a drink of water and looked at the back of his head. "What happened?" he asked, as he poured water on his handkerchief and held it to Rice's head.

The cool water began to clear Rice's head. "I'm not sure, sir. I remember walking out into the field to look for the horses. Lelia was waiting in the shade by the creek. The next thing I knew I woke up here."

"QUICK MR. PATTON, OVER HERE!" one of the men shouted, rushing out of the woods.

Patton jumped up and ran across the field, leaving Rice struggling to get up again, but he was still too weak and dizzy to stand. "WHAT'S HAPPENED TO LELIA?" he cried out, when one of the men ran to his horse.

"She's been attacked over by the creek. She's still alive, but she's real bad. I'm going back to the barn to get a wagon and send for the doctor," he shouted, as he galloped away.

Determined to see Lelia, Rice forced himself to stand up and walk towards the woods, but after only a few steps, the pain exploded through his head. In the dimming light, the ground tilted upward and he fell forward, blood now flowing out of the wound again, covering his face and mouth. When he woke up the next time, he was surprised and confused to see that it was his own father who was wiping his face and bandaging his head. "How'd you get here, Pop?" he whispered, reaching for the canteen of water.

"I rode over to the Pattons' looking for you when it got so late. Got there just as they were leaving with the wagon to come back out here, so I rode along," Eli said.

"Pop, how bad is Lelia?" Rice asked, his voice cracking.

"They're bringing her out now," Eli said, pointing to the cluster of men surrounding John Patton, as he carried Lelia wrapped in blankets. All the farmhands stood quietly with their heads down while Patton gently placed her in the wagon.

"Let's see if we can get you up, son," Eli said, tucking his arm around Rice's back and armpit. Slowly, he pulled him up, and they made their way to the wagon, but it was clear that Rice was too weak to ride his horse.

"How is she John?" Eli asked, bracing Rice up against the side of the wagon.

Patton shook his head. "She's alive, but she's badly hurt. I've stopped the bleeding that I could see, but it was such a brutal attack, I don't know about what's happening inside her. I just hope the doctor is at the house when we get back. Maybe you could start saying some of your prayers for her on the ride back."

"I've already been praying for both our children," Eli said, still holding Rice up. "He's lost a lot of blood and is too weak to ride. If you don't mind, I'll put him in the wagon too, all right?"

Patton glared at Rice. "I can see you're hurt, but it's nothing like my girl. I blame you for letting this happen. Your health is no concern of mine, but if you need to be in the wagon, then go ahead. Just don't think of touching my daughter. I'll be watching you."

Anger and pain and the very real fear that Lelia was lost to him forever welled up inside Rice, but all he said was, "Yes sir," and allowed the men to lift him into the wagon next to Lelia.

The trip back to the house didn't take long. Eli and John Patton rode together, saying nothing, each lost in the misery of how close they had come to losing their children that day. Eli thanked God that they were still alive, while Patton seethed and imagined himself killing whoever did it. In the wagon, Rice turned his head sideways, to stare at Lelia's face, streaked with blood and dirt, shrouded in the blankets. With the clattering of the horses and the creaking of the wagon wheels, no one could hear him as he spoke softly to her, telling her how sorry he was, how much he loved her, and assuring her that everything would be all right. For most of the ride, the sky was completely dark with only an occasional sliver of moonlight. No one saw that Lelia had turned her head and was staring back at Rice and moving her lips, or more importantly that she slipped her hand out of the blanket to take hold of his hand.

———

## 21

Wednesday June 9, 1863

Rice is better. Harri was able to stitch up his head wound and except for the terrible headaches which come on when he moves around too much, he's almost normal. He's worried sick about Lelia and so far the Pattons aren't talking to us. Nerva is talking more, but says she doesn't remember what happened at the Johnsons' or how she got here. I don't believe her. Lieutenant Hunt stopped by late yesterday with two soldiers. They chose three young American Saddlebreds, transferred their saddles and left us with three pitifully worn down Morgans to care for. Said they'd be back soon. The whole exchange took less than an hour. If the Devil was watching, he kept it to himself. He's just biding his time and waiting for the worst possible moment to use this partnership to his advantage. God help us.

Closing his diary, Eli tried to clear his mind and focus on his Sunday sermon. It was becoming harder and harder each week to come up with a meaningful message that brought comfort and strength to his struggling congregations. This Sunday he was due to preach at the Jonesborough Presbyterian Church, where a tight knit group of Union supporters worshiped. Some of them had been stripped of their properties as punishment for passing around a petition, urging East Tennesseans to break away and form a separate state after Tennessee became part of the Confederacy. Now these old refined families were living in groups in ramshackle lean-tos in the woods or along the streams. Preaching to them about the mercy of God only reinforced their anger and bitterness. He was thinking that it might be the right time to revisit the Old Testament's Book of Job. This passionate study of the faith of the innocent when subjected to unbearable suffering would certainly apply now. As he began writing his notes, the sound of loud, angry voices came from the front of the house. Harriet and Nerva were over at the store, so he rushed out to see who was there.

Rice and John Patton were facing off on the front porch. "It's not right that you won't let me see her," Rice said loudly.

"I'll decide what's right for her," Patton growled, pushing his finger into Rice's chest.

"What's all this?" Eli asked, opening the front door wide. "I'm glad you're here, John. Come on in," he said, stepping back as Patton pushed past Rice whose face was dark purple. "You sit down for a bit son, or maybe go over to the barn and see how Morgan and Ford are doing without you," Eli said quietly, closing the door.

Rice scowled. "This is my fight, Pop. I'll wait right here." But Eli had already turned away.

"Let's go back to my library, John," Eli said, leading him down the hallway and closing the door behind them. "How is she? We're all worried, and Rice can't think of anything else."

Patton settled into one of the arm chairs, facing the desk. "The doctor thinks she'll recover physically over time, but emotionally she may never be the same," he sighed.

"Has she been able to say what happened?" Eli asked.

"About the same thing Rice told us," he answered quietly. "They'd been picnicking on the rocks and then they couldn't find their horses when they were ready to leave. Lelia waited at the edge of the woods by the creek where it was cool, while Rice walked out into the field looking for them. She lost sight of him, and then out of nowhere a big man knocked her to the ground from behind and pushed rags and dirt into her mouth. He tied her hands behind her and held her down." Patton looked away, his eyes welling up with tears and his throat too tight to speak. "And then he raped my little girl," he whispered.

Eli stood up, walked around the desk, and put his hands on Patton's shoulders. "I'm so sorry John. That poor girl—what can we do to help her, help all of you through this?"

Patton wiped his face and cleared his throat. "Lelia is asking for Rice, and I've been saying no, because I'm so angry with him for letting this happen. My wife, Orpha thinks I'm wrong. She thinks Rice will help Lelia recover."

Eli went back to his chair. "I know you're angry, John. I suppose it's natural for you to blame Rice because he was out there with her. But I think, for Lelia's sake, you're going to have to put aside your anger and find a way to forgive him."

"Putting it aside is one thing, forgiving is another," Patton snapped, standing up. "But I'll ask him to come over," he sighed.

"One thing John," Eli said. "We need to tell our neighbors about this second attack, again on private property. We don't have to detail what happened to Lelia, but it's important that they know something else has happened. Doesn't it seem strange to you that neither one of these terrible invasions has been about stealing something? It's more like pure evil running rampant, and it's not just one person."

"There had to have been at least two of them when they got

Lelia and Rice while they were separated," Patton agreed.

"Maybe we should go out there and look around in the daylight," Eli suggested.

"Sheriff Hawkins is coming over tomorrow afternoon. It might help if you and Rice joined us. He's going to want to talk to Rice anyway," Patton said, walking to the front door.

"We'll be glad to help," Eli agreed as they reached the porch where Rice was waiting. Eli shook Patton's hand. "Until tomorrow then, John, I'll leave you two to talk."

———

## 22

"What's wrong with you two?" Harriet asked at dinner. "You're not talking and you've hardly eaten anything."

Eli smiled at her. "Sorry Harri. John Patton was here this afternoon. He wants Rice and me to come over tomorrow and meet with Sheriff Hawkins."

"Are you up to that Rice?" Harriet asked, frowning.

"I'm fine Mother," Rice answered angrily, pushing back his chair. "I'm going upstairs."

Harriet sighed. "Did I say something wrong?"

"No Harri, it's not that," Eli said, reaching for her hand. "Rice blames himself for what happened to Lelia, and even worse, John Patton does too. He's only letting Rice see her because Orpha is insisting he will help Lelia get better."

Harriet stared hard at Eli. "What did happen to Lelia?"

"It's very bad," he said, looking away from her. He couldn't manage to face her as he described what Patton had said happened to Lelia.

Afterwards, Harriet sat quietly with her hands covering her face, until finally she whispered, "And Rice knows all of this?"

"John talked to him this afternoon and he asked him to see her," Eli said, putting his arm around her shoulders.

"Those poor children," Harriet sobbed. "They're just getting started in life and now they have to overcome this. Just where do you think God was when this happened, Eli?"

"I believe God was with them, keeping them alive," he answered wearily.

Harriet moved away from him and started clearing the dishes. "Just like he was at the Johnsons'—right? But he didn't keep them alive did he?"

Harriet's darkness filled Eli's heart with fear and sadness. He wondered whether or not anything at all he did would ever make any difference in the world. "No, he didn't and I don't know why," he said quietly, walking out the back door and away from the house and Harri's anger.

———

## *23*

Early the next morning, Lieutenant Hunt and two soldiers rode up to the barn. Eli and Rice had just brought out the last of the horses from the stalls. Morgan and Ford had already turned the ones that had spent the night in the paddock out into the pasture to graze. "Good morning Reverend Marsh," Hunt called. "We thought we could swap off our mounts for some more of your horses. That worked out well the other day."

"You can take your pick of these," Eli said, pointing to the paddock. "We just brought them out."

Hunt selected two Morgans and a Chestnut this time, and the transfer of saddles and gear was done quickly. "We'll be back again in a few days," he said, preparing to ride away."

Eli nodded. "I believe our agreement was $150 for each horse. When do you think you'll be able to pay for the six you've already taken?" he asked.

Hunt smiled nervously. "Don't worry. The Major will settle up with you next time. How are our horses doing?"

"It's gonna take a while," Rice said. "They're pretty worn out and these look even worse," he added, pointing to the latest drop-offs.

Hunt looked worried. "Do you think they'll be ready by August?"

"Maybe. Is that when you'll be needing them back?" Rice asked.

"Just do the best you can," Hunt said, turning to leave.

"Did you see anyone on the road, Lieutenant?" Eli called after him.

Hunt shook his head. "We stay off the roads as much as possible."

"Just wondering—Rice and I are riding over towards Greeneville this afternoon and we don't want any trouble," Eli said.

"That's why we stick to the woods. By the way, what happened to your head Rice?" Hunt asked.

"Got knocked out from behind a few days ago over at a farm near here," Rice answered, staring at Hunt and the other soldiers. "Y'all happen to hear anything about that?"

Hunt shook his head and turned to leave. "How would we know about it? We don't spend time talking to many folks around here. You be careful out there today."

Eli and Rice watched them ride down the drive. "Where do you think they're camped, Pop?" Rice asked quietly.

"I don't know, son. But it can't be too far away, given the way they stop by here so easily. "And did you notice—their horses hadn't even broken a sweat, so they hadn't ridden long at all."

Rice stood thinking. "I'm gonna ride up to the top of the ridge behind the barn. They could be camped just down on the other side by the stream—they could be right here on our land, Pop!"

"You going now?" Eli worried. "Because we'll need to leave for the Pattons' by noon."

"I'll be back in plenty of time," Rice said, saddling his horse.

"Just keep your eyes open," Eli called, as Rice rode away. "You don't need another crack on the head," he said mostly to himself.

———

24

Racing across the pasture with the wind whipping his face, Rice felt energized and like himself again. The ache in his head was better, and now he couldn't wait to see Lelia that afternoon. He needed to reassure her that no matter what had happened—no matter how bad it was—he loved her even more, and their life together would go on. When she took his hand in the wagon, he knew she was still his and he felt certain he could make her well.

After about twenty minutes, he reached the base of the ridge and found the zigzag path to the top. Even though they owned the land on the other side down to the stream and woods below, he rarely had the time to ride there. Sometimes Eli rode this way going back and forth to Afton, because it was faster than the road in good weather. When he neared the top of the ridge, Rice got off his horse and walked quietly the rest of the way, reaching the moss covered rocks at the top. Below was the lush green valley brimming with wild daisies and black eyed susans, and a lazy stream running through it. Beyond were dense woods which stretched to the next ridge and the boundary of the Marsh property.

Rice had often thought this sweet little hidden valley would be a perfect place to build a house and start a life of his own. But there was nothing tranquil about the site he saw now. What the Hell, they're right here he said out loud, as he watched large groups of Union soldiers rushing in and out of the woods. Pop won't believe this he thought, as he turned and hurried back down the path.

Eli and Harriet were sitting on the front porch when Rice rode up. He jumped off his horse and ran up the steps. "I was right Pop!" he panted. "Union soldiers are camped right over the ridge in the woods by the stream."

Alarmed, Eli and Harriet both stood up. "How many?" Eli asked.

Rice shrugged. "They're in the trees, so I couldn't really tell, but I saw a lot of movement. I think it could be a fair sized unit."

Eli rubbed his forehead. "I just rode that way at the beginning of the month and there was no one there. Must have just happened."

"What does it mean for us, Eli?" Harriet asked.

"It's not good, Harri. Even though we had no idea they were there, we could still be arrested for harboring the enemy—not to mention our horse trading arrangement. Our best hope is that they move on farther west towards Knoxville soon," Eli said.

"Couldn't we just ask them to leave?" Harriet pleaded.

Eli walked down the steps towards Gray who was saddled and waiting. "I'll try to talk to them tomorrow. Right now Rice and I need to get over to the Pattons'."

"Let me just clean up a little for Lelia," Rice said, hurrying into the house and taking off his shirt.

"It's good he's worrying about making a good impression on Lelia," Harriet mused. "That poor girl is probably worried to death about seeing him. I'm going to cut some roses for him to bring to her," she added, going around to the side of the house. When Eli and Rice left, they both had bundles of pink and white roses hanging from their saddles. "Tell Lelia, I'm keeping her in my thoughts." Harriet said.

"Stay close to the house or store while we're gone. Morgan and Ford will be watching," Eli said.

Harriet nodded and waved. She looked up toward the barn where Morgan was standing with his rifle, and across the road she could see Ford and Nerva sitting outside the Bee. His rifle was propped next to him. "Marsh martial law," she said under her breath. "Will this ever be over?"

---

## 25

Eli and Rice arrived at the Pattons' just as Sheriff Hawkins and two of his men rode up. John Patton walked out to meet them. "Thank you for coming. Let's get this over with," he said, mounting his horse.

"I'll catch up with you," Rice said, jumping down from his horse and taking the flowers to the house. "Give these to Lelia and tell her I'll be back soon," he said, handing them to the houseman. Quickly he caught up with the group, as they galloped across the fields and reached the woods and creek in a short time.

"Why don't you walk us through what happened, Rice," Hawkins suggested.

So Rice led them into the woods and pointed out where he and Lelia had left the horses and the boulder where they sat. "Our horses were either standing in the creek or grazing right at the edge of the woods. So we were surprised they were gone when we were ready to leave. I left Lelia right here while I went to look for them," he said, pointing to the matted grass and mud.

"And this is where you found her, John?" Hawkins asked.

Unbearable pain etched across Patton's face, as he nodded his head. "She was face down, hands tied behind her back, and barely breathing," he whispered.

Hawkins knelt down to inspect the ground and then asked Rice to show him where he had been hit. Out in the open field, Rice found the spot where he remembered coming to. The grass was still trampled down there too. "So you didn't see or hear anyone the whole time you two were on the creek boulder or out here?" he asked.

"No one," Rice answered.

"All right then, you all go on back to the house. My men and I will look around here for a while and meet you back there later," Hawkins said, motioning to Patton and Eli and Rice. Both fathers objected and wanted to stay, but Hawkins was firm, saying they could move much faster without any more help from the families. Meanwhile, Rice was very happy to be released, so he could get back to see Lelia. The three men rode in silence and when they reached the house, Patton frowned and locked his hand around Rice's good arm and growled, "Lelia is waiting for you. Don't stay too long."

Annoyed with Patton's tone, Rice shook his arm loose and nodded as he hurried into the house.

Patton sighed and pointed to the side garden. "Let's have a smoke, Eli. I feel a hundred years old."

Eli laughed. "I know. I've been feeling that way myself lately. I used to believe that with God's help I was in control of my life. But now it seems to be spinning away from me and I can't see what's ahead."

———

# 26

Lelia's mother Orpha met Rice when he raced into the house. "Thank goodness you're here," she said, smiling. "Lelia has been asking for you for days."

Rice took off his hat. "How is she Mrs. Patton?"

"She'll be much better when she sees you," Orpha said, taking his hand. "She's already told me that you two want to be married. I hope you haven't changed your mind," she whispered, staring into his eyes.

Rice stood completely still. "Of course not," he stammered, his face turning bright red. "But after all that's happened, I wanted to be sure she still felt the same way."

Orpha relaxed and smiled again. "She wants to know that you feel the same way too. This was terrible for her. There's no getting around the fact that she's a changed person, but she's strong and she loves you. With your help, she'll be able to start putting this behind her and move on."

"No one else knows that we want to marry. I'll have to tell

my parents and then I'll talk to Mr. Patton, but he's not happy with me at all," Rice said, looking down.

Orpha sighed. "I promise he will give his blessing. Lelia is in the sitting room upstairs. Now go on up and see her."

Lelia sat propped up against pillows on a sofa. Her eyes were closed and her dark hair hung loosely down around her shoulders. The cuts and bruises on her face were beginning to fade. Only the dark shadows under her eyes betrayed the pain and sadness she had been enduring. "Lelia, I'm here," Rice said quietly, as she opened her swollen eyes and held out her arms to him. Kneeling down, he melted into her embrace, and they held each other tightly.

Finally he sat back and took her hand. "I will never forgive myself for what happened to you."

Lelia felt his bandaged head. "This wasn't your fault. You were hurt too, Rice," she whispered.

"IT WAS MY FAULT!" he said angrily. "When I find out who did this, I promise you, I will kill them."

Lelia put her fingers on his lips. "Shhh—don't talk like that. Tell me Rice, will you still have me, now that this happened?"

Rice put his arm around her shoulders. "Can we just get married right now? I want to be with you now, right next to you for the rest of my life."

Tears slipped down Lelia's cheeks, but she giggled at the same time. "I love you Rice. Just give me a few weeks, until I feel better."

Orpha tapped on the door. "Sheriff Hawkins is here. He wonders if you are up to talking to him."

Lelia took a deep breath. "All right Mama, tell him to come up, but I want Rice to stay here with me."

Orpha frowned. "Your Daddy is going to want to be with you too."

Rice pulled a chair over next to Lelia and took her hand again as Hawkins, Patton and Eli came into the sitting room. Each

one greeted Lelia, and Hawkins apologized for bothering her. "I promise this won't take too long. Your Daddy and Rice here have told me what happened. I'd like to hear from you what you remember."

Lelia nodded and described the same events just as Rice had earlier.

"Can you tell me anything at all about who attacked you?" he asked gently.

"He was behind me the whole time, so I never saw his face, but he seemed very big. All I saw were dark sleeved arms pushing into the creek bank."

"That's all?" Hawkins asked, sounding disappointed.

Lelia nodded, tears sliding down her face. "But just before I passed out, he said something like—See how you like being with that one-arm Southern kid after this," she sobbed.

Silent anger and shock filled the room. The men stared grimly at each other, ashamed of their maleness in the presence of this beautiful, soft-spoken young woman. Orpha moved to Lelia's side. "I think that's enough gentlemen," she said, motioning them toward the door.

"Yes, thank you Lelia, if you think of anything else, please let me know. We'll do our best to find the men who did this," Hawkins said, as he left the room.

Rice kissed Lelia on her cheek. "I'll come back up before I leave."

Downstairs in the parlor, the men huddled together and talked in hushed voices. "Goddamned Yankee soldiers did this Sheriff," Patton sputtered, his face purple with rage. "Right here on my land, they attacked my daughter! What are you going to do about it? Is there a Union camp around here and I don't know about it?"

"Try to calm down, John," Hawkins said. "No one heard her say it was a Union soldier. The only thing she saw were dark sleeves. Look around you in this room. We're all wearing dark sleeves, even you."

Patton sank down in a chair. "What about what she remembered he said about Rice—calling him a one-arm Southern kid? No one from around here would say that. It has to be Yankees you're looking for," he seethed.

Hawkins frowned. "I don't know anything about the Union setting up camps here, but the talk is they're gearing up to try to reinforce Knoxville soon, so they could be around. I agree with you that no one from around here would talk about Rice like that, but we didn't find one thing in the field or woods that would point to a Union soldier."

Eli and Rice exchanged worried stares. "Do you think there's any connection between this attack and the Johnson murders?" Eli asked.

"Possibly," Hawkins said. "But what's their motive? It's not robbery. Are these just treacherous men, out to do random, evil deeds and why here?"

"That idea doesn't work for me," Patton growled. "Everyone knows the Johnsons were abolitionists and Union sympathizers. Mack went around openly cursing the Confederacy. That's why they were killed—to shut them up and stop their do-good railroading. Their deaths have nothing to do with those slimey Yankee soldiers who attacked Lelia and Rice. Mark my words."

Uneasy silence fell over the room. Rice was thinking that this crazy man was going to be his father-in-law and he had to get along with him, even though he didn't like him at all. At the same time, Eli concluded that Patton knew something about what happened to the Johnsons. He and Rice needed to stay far away from him or they would be at great risk, if Patton found out about the horse trading and the Union camp on their land.

Hawkins stood up to leave. "John if you know something I should know, I trust you'll tell me. You could be putting innocent families at risk by staying quiet." But Patton said nothing. So Hawkins added, "Reverend, it's getting late. You and Rice should get on the road too. You seem to be caught up in both these crimes, so best to watch yourselves and Mrs. Marsh."

"Thank you Sheriff. We'll be careful," Eli said, walking out the door with him. "By the way, Nerva is talking, but she says she doesn't remember what happened over there."

"Do you believe her?" Hawkins asked.

"Not really," Eli said shaking his head. "She's warming up to us though, so maybe she'll tell us more, when she's not so afraid."

Rice ran up the stairs to say good-bye to Lelia, but Orpha stopped him in the hall. "She's sleeping. I'll tell her good-bye for you. Come back soon, Rice. She needs you."

Rice nodded and promised to be back in a day or two. Then he joined Eli, and they said good-bye to John Patton. "Thank you for letting me see Lelia, sir. If it's all right with you, I'd like to come back in a day or two."

"Yes, she seems better when you are here," Patton grumbled and turned away from them.

"Let's get home, son, before something else troubling happens," Eli said, his face grim.

———

# 27

Sheriff Hawkins was waiting on the road when Rice and Eli reached the entrance to the Pattons' drive. "Another moment please Reverend," he called when they rode up. "Did you finish moving all those horses over from the Johnson place?"

"Yes sir, we did," Rice answered.

Hawkins whistled and pushed his hat back. "So they're all at your barn?"

"Well, we left that one dead black in the stall," Eli sighed. "And a couple of Confederate soldiers helped themselves to two horses, while we were resting in the creek on the way home."

Hawkins frowned. "Just two lone soldiers?"

Eli nodded. "That's right. Never saw anyone else, and the truth is those two were so dirty and hungry, we took them for runaways."

Hawkins agreed. "You're probably right about that. Both armies are having problems with boys just walking away. Here's the thing Reverend. Colonel Reese Jones, who's in charge of the Confederate troops over in Greeneville, asked me about the Johnson horses. He seemed to know it was a big stable."

"And you told him we had them?" Eli asked.

"I did. Don't be surprised if he stops by to have a look at them. He wants to add to his supply."

"Do you think he's planning to help himself or offer us a price?" Rice asked. "'Cause we hear they've been taking pretty much whatever they want from folks."

Hawkins shrugged. "I hope he makes you a fair offer, but it could go the other way. Anyway, I just wanted to let you know," he said, waving his hand as he turned and rode away with his men.

Eli and Rice turned and rode in the other direction towards the farm. "Now what, Pop?" Rice asked.

Eli shook his head. "The Devil has started playing with us, just as I thought he would. We'll just have to hope that our Union partners don't show up at the same time as this Colonel Jones."

"What'll we do if that happens?" Rice asked.

Eli tried to sound calm even though his heart was beating wildly at the very thought. "I have to hope they would be gentlemen about a chance meeting at our barn and leave it at that. But if it went badly, we might lose everything and probably be arrested by someone!"

Seeing how upset his father was, Rice kept quiet for a while as the whole idea of losing their home and all the horses sank in. What would happen to them? Would they end up living in one of those lean-to shacks somewhere? He couldn't imagine it. Trying to sound practical, he said, "We're surely going to have to keep those poor Union horses out of sight, Pop. They're in such pitiful shape. Anyone with any horse sense could maybe figure out where they came from."

Eli was lost in his own gloomy thoughts and didn't answer Rice. They rode the rest of the way in silence, both trying to imagine what the coming days would bring. Rice thought of Lelia and their hope for a future life together. Eli was filled with dread that the life he and Harri knew would end, and they might be lost forever. As hard as he tried, he couldn't escape the doom he felt. When they reached the barn, Eli said quietly, "I think I'll ride over the ridge to that camp tomorrow and have a word with Major Carrigan—ask him to be more careful about sending his men over to our house."

Rice nodded. "Good idea."

Harriet and Nerva had dinner waiting for them at the house. To her surprise, Harriet was enjoying Nerva's company and house-keeping help. For the first time in her married life, she was freed of the constant cleaning and cooking, and able to concentrate on the store and her gardens without feeling guilty. And she liked taking Nerva under her wing and bringing her back to life. With Nerva cleaning up after dinner, Harriet joined Eli and Rice on the porch that evening. They weren't making any conversation, so she finally asked, "How's Lelia, Rice?"

"She's doing all right thank God," he said, standing up to face his parents. "We want to get married. I'm going to ask Mr. Patton for his permission."

Harriet threw her arms around Rice, and Eli put his arm around him too and shook his hand. "This is wonderful news!" she cried. "We've been hoping all along it would be Lelia, haven't we, Eli."

"She'll make a wonderful wife for you son," Eli agreed. "I just hope John Patton doesn't give you a hard time when you talk to him. He's very worked up right now."

"I know Pop. I'm hoping he'll see this as good news and the best thing for Lelia."

"I'm so excited for you two!" Harriet laughed. "When do you think you'll set the date ?"

"Lelia and I haven't talked about that yet, but it probably won't be for a few months. She needs time to feel well again. Maybe sometime in the fall unless the War gets in the way," Rice said, looking at Eli who shook his head and put his finger to his lips. He had decided not to tell Harriet about the possibility of a confrontation between the armies over the horses right here on their farm.

Completely missing the silent exchange between Rice and Eli, Harriet continued on excitedly, "And you'll be bringing her back here to live?"

"I guess we'll have to live here until we can build a place of our own. Will that be all right with you?" Rice asked.

Harriet smiled. "Of course, it'll be a bit of a step-down for Lelia from that big house, but Nerva and I can take care of her."

"All right then. I'll go over there Sunday afternoon," Rice said, going inside, hoping his talk with John Patton would go as smoothly as this one had.

Harrriet clapped her hands quietly. "At last, some good news!" she exclaimed, taking Eli's hand.

"I know Harri. We've been praying for this for a long time. They deserve every happiness. I just hope the War doesn't get in their way."

"Don't be so gloomy, Eli. People fall in love and marry even in war time," Harriet scolded him. "Rice isn't going to be drafted, so they won't be forced apart. Why shouldn't they find some happiness for themselves?"

"Of course, you're right," Eli agreed. "But I'm worried that John might put up a fight, because he is such a staunch Confederate supporter, and we clearly are not."

Harriet sniffed. "Orpha will never let him refuse. She wants this marriage as much as we do. She'll work on him. You'll see."

Eli chuckled. "She's a forceful woman for sure, but we still need to be very careful around John. If he gets wind of our horse trading arrangement, he could make our lives miserable."

"Can we just be happy about this and not look for all the worst possibilities?" Harriet pleaded.

Eli took both her hands and pulled her up out of her chair and twirled her around the porch. "I'm sorry, Harri. Let's go upstairs and be nothing but happy for the future Mr. and Mrs. Marsh," he said, smiling.

———

## 28

*June 11, 1863*

*A quiet night thank God. We all needed the rest. Riding over to the Union camp early this morning. Need to tell Major Carrigan and Lieutenant Hunt not to come to the barn again. Too much risk of running into Confederates looking for horses too. Happy for Rice and Lelia. They're bery brave to be planning a future together in such bad times. Their spirit astounds me.*

It was barely light when Eli rode Gray out of the barn. The horses in the paddock were stirring, anxious to get out into the fields. He reached the top of the ridge behind the pastures in a short time.

Looking down through the mist, he could see low flickering camp fires in the woods on the far side of the fields below, just as Rice had said. He slowly zigzagged down the slope to the valley and crossed the stream to the edge of the woods. Two young soldiers carrying raised rifles appeared from behind the dense trees and walked out to meet him. "Stop sir. What do you want here?" one demanded.

Eli introduced himself. "I'm Reverend Marsh and this is my land. I'm looking for Major Carrigan or Lieutenant Hunt."

"What makes you think they're here?" the other sentry asked.

"They've been to my house several times. I'm sure if you tell them I'm here, they'll want to talk to me," he said calmly.

"Wait here," the first sentry said, going back into the woods while the other one continued to keep his gun pointed at Eli.

Staring into the woods, Eli could make out the outlines of a sea of low-lying tents and flickering fires, but not much activity. He guessed they were keeping the horses on the other side of the woods at the base of the next ridge. He wondered how on earth they had found this little hidden valley. It was certainly a good place to hide, but a terrible place to get caught. The Confederates could easily box them in and there would be no way out. Surely they had realized that and weren't planning to stay here long.

With no sound, the sentry reappeared. "Major Carrigan wants you to come to his tent. You can leave your horse here."

Eli smiled. "I think I'll bring him in with me. He gets worried if he can't see me," he said, following the sentry into the woods.

Seated at a small table in front of a tent, Major Carrigan stood up and shook Eli's hand. "Welcome Reverend. You found us," he said, smiling and pointing to a stool.

Eli tied Gray to a tent stake and sat down. "Thank you for seeing me."

"First time in a military camp?" Carrigan asked, offering him a cigar.

Eli nodded. "It's very impressive how organized it is," he

said, waving off the cigar and holding up his pipe instead.

"So how did you find us?" Carrigan asked.

Eli stretched his legs. "Rice got curious after the last time Lieutenant Hunt came by to trade horses and then disappeared so quickly. He took a ride up to the top of the ridge and saw your camp."

"That easy!" Carrigan said, frowning.

Eli sighed. "This is Rice's valley. He's been coming here all his life. He's hoping to marry soon, and I think he's got an idea to build a house right over there where the slope plateaus a bit," he said, pointing through the trees.

Carrigan stared off into the trees. "I hope that works out for him. A lot of us here have hopes and dreams too, but we've had to put them off to serve our country.

Eli cleared his throat. "It's a terrible sacrifice all of you are making. Rice and I wish we could do more to help, believe me. That's really why I'm here. I came to warn you. The Confederates are interested in our horses as well. They'll be coming to the barn anytime now. You can't just show up there anymore. It's too dangerous for everyone."

Carrigan stood up and paced back and forth. "I appreciate you coming out here to tell me, Reverend. How do they know about your horses?"

Eli stood up too. "I think I should tell you more about our horses, Major. Remember I told you we had taken in about twenty-five horses and mules from the stable of a friend who had passed away?"

Carrigan nodded. "I remember thinking that seemed very generous of you considering how overcrowded your barn is."

"Generous or very foolish—time will tell," Eli mused. "Anyway, the horses came from a farm up the road from us owned by Mack and Mary Johnson. Their two boys were drafted into the Confederate army and later died at Vicksburg. The Johnsons were staunch abolitionists and Union supporters. They were devastated when the boys were drafted, but their hearts were completely broken when the boys died. Mack loved his horses, but he wasn't caring for them properly and he had lost the will to even try. We agreed to take them, but everything had changed when Rice and I went to get them."

Carrigan sat back down and listened closely as Eli described the gruesome scene at the Johnson barn. "Sheriff Hawkins came over from Greeneville to investigate and he agreed that we should take the horses as planned, since there was no one there to care for them. I saw him again yesterday, and he told me the Confederate Colonel Reese Jones, who's in charge in Greeneville, asked him about the Johnson horses. Hawkins told him we had moved them to our barn."

"So what happened to the Johnsons over here was news even in Greeneville?" Carrigan asked.

Eli nodded. "Absolutely Major—For one thing Mack Johnson was a cousin of Andrew Johnson. They weren't particularly close, but anything about that family is news around here. But probably more important is the fact that we aren't used to violent crimes in these parts. People are bound to be talking about it because they're worried and scared for their families."

"And there's still no idea about who did it?" Carrigan asked.

Eli shook his head. "Nothing yet, but there's been another attack," he said and then described what had happened to Rice and Lelia. "So Major, besides the War bearing down on us, we're all wondering who will be attacked next on our own property minding our own business."

The two men sat staring at each other. "Two very different crimes—I doubt they're connected," Carrigan finally said. "Of course, that makes it more worrisome for you folks, because now you might be looking for more than one criminal. You know Reverend, sometimes people use war as an excuse to settle scores or take advantage of others and it gets blamed on soldiers."

Eli agreed. "Some folks are thinking that way too. In any case, I've got to get back. If it's all right with you Major, it's probably best for us to bring horses to you by crossing the ridge from now on. That way we'd be on our land the whole time just herding horses if anyone gets suspicious."

Surprised, Carrigan jerked his head back. "You'd be willing to do that?"

Eli smiled. "As long as Colonel Jones doesn't come over and take all our horses, I'm still up for trading with you."

The Major extended his hand. "Thank you Reverend. It's a different arrangement, but let's try it and see how it goes."

"It'll probably be Rice and one of our hands riding over with three or four horses at a time," Eli said.

"And we can count on you choosing strong ones for us?" Carrigan asked, as he walked Eli and Gray out of the woods.

Eli smiled. "You'll have to trust us on that."

"Wait here for a moment Reverend. I have something for you in my tent," Carrigan said, as he turned and hurried back into the woods while Eli mounted Gray. When he came back out, he pressed an envelope into Eli's hand. "This should make us even until next time."

Without opening it, Eli tucked it inside his coat, "Right Major, until then."

Carrigan watched Eli ride across the valley to the base of the ridge. "Find Lieutenant Hunt and ask him to come to my tent," he said to one of the sentries.

When Hunt came in, the Major related what Eli had told him about the Confederates' interest in the horses. "So new plan— the Marshes are going to bring the horses to us from now on. Marsh is a good man. He's trying to prevent a confrontation on his land over the horses that might turn into something ugly. We've put him in a bad spot."

Hunt frowned. "I don't know sir. How's this going to work?"

"We agreed to try it and see how it goes. Clearly we can't go over there anymore. They'll start bringing us some more horses next week. We'll most likely be dealing with Rice on this. You should have some ready to hand over to him in exchange. How many more do we need to rehabilitate?"

"I'm thinking maybe a dozen would do it," Hunt answered.

Carrigan exhaled. "Good—Hopefully the Confederates don't clean them out right away, before we have what we need. That's all, Lieutenant."

When Eli reached the top of the ridge, he paused and looked back down across the valley. He was relieved to see that in the late morning sun the Union camp had become invisible, shrouded by the woods. He wished he had had the courage to ask the Major how long they planned to camp there. But despite their friendly business arrangement, he felt that Carrigan wouldn't share information with him unless it suited him. The only clue to when they would leave had come from Lieutenant Hunt when he asked Rice if their horses could be ready by August. He and Harri would have to hold on to that timing and pray that their involvement with the Union army remained secret.

As he descended the ridge down to the pastures, he took in the beauty of their farm, framed by the Smokies in the distance, with all the horses grazing in the pastures and the corn growing tall in the field by the barn. All the summer vegetables would start coming in soon, and Harri and Nerva would get busy putting them up for the winter. He wondered how adding Lelia to their household would affect Harri, and if their house was big enough for two strong willed women sharing Rice's attention. It would be best for everyone if Rice and Lelia could build their own house to start their lives together. But building anything now seemed out of the question. They were all on hold until the War was over.

———

# 29

Anxious to know how the meeting went, Rice rode out to meet his father when he saw him start down the ridge. "How'd it go Pop?" he called when he got close enough.

"Not bad. You and Morgan or Ford will be delivering the horses to them from now on. You can start next week," Eli said. "They agree that if anyone notices, it will look like we're just moving some of our horses to the back valley to graze."

Rice nodded in agreement. "That's a smart plan. What's the camp like?"

"Very tight and organized. You really can't see it until you get inside the woods," Eli said. "I can't imagine they'll stay there too long. It's a good hiding place, but if the Confederates find them, there will be no way out. We've got to be very careful that no one else knows about this, and you know who I mean," he added, staring at Rice.

Rice frowned. "Don't worry Pop. I won't tell anyone—certainly not Lelia. Her father would personally bring Confederate soldiers over here if he knew."

Relieved that Rice understood about John Patton, Eli breathed a sigh of relief, but he worried about him not being able to be totally honest with his future wife. "Keeping secrets is no way to start a marriage, son. Nothing but pain and heartache come from it. But I do agree with you about the wrath of John Patton, and what he would do, if he knew about what we're doing. Let's hope Major Carrigan and his unit move on West before you and Lelia marry."

Rice nodded. "Mother gave me Grandma Burkhart's wedding rings. She wants me to use them. What do you think, Pop?"

Eli smiled. "I'm not surprised at all. Your mother really wants this marriage to work for you and Lelia. If she's giving you those beautiful rings, then she's investing in you and the future of our family."

Rice laughed nervously. "I'm hoping to talk to Mr. Patton on Sunday and get that over with."

Eli shook his head. "Sunday's no good. I have to preach in Jonesborough, so I need you to be here. You'll have to wait until next week."

Disappointment framed Rice's face and sarcasm tinged his voice. "That's right. I forgot. You're not just a farmer, a storekeeper and a horse trader. You work for God too. Do you think He gets jealous of all your other jobs?"

Eli looked sideways at his son, surprised by his acid tone. "It's the life that's been given to me, Rice. All I can do is try to make it work. But I have to admit, I'm getting spread pretty thin these days."

They rode the rest of the way in silence, but when they reached the barn, Rice put his arm on Eli's, "Sorry Pop, I was just thinking of myself. I'll stay here Sunday. You go ahead home while I take care of the horses. Mother's probably got lunch ready."

Nerva was setting the table when Eli walked into the house. Although she seemed to be completely recovered, she still frightened easily and she jumped back when she saw him. "It's okay Nerva. It's just me," Eli said quietly. "Where's Mrs. Marsh?"

Nerva kept her head down. "She still over at the Bee. She be here directly."

"Thank you. I'm going to wash up," Eli said, climbing the stairs.

Harriet found him as he was drying off and kissed him on the cheek. "How's the horse war going?"

Eli smiled, happy to see her in a good mood. "It's still happening. The Major's unit is very cozy over there in our woods."

She pursed her lips at this news. "Any chance they might leave soon?"

"Maybe," Eli said. "The main thing is they won't be coming here anymore. The Major agrees it's too risky."

"Thank God he listened to you," she said. "Now if we can just keep the Confederates away too."

Eli shrugged. "I doubt it Harri. They can go wherever they want and take whatever they need anytime. We've been very lucky so far that they've mainly stayed away from us out here in the country. But they're making life pretty miserable in the towns. If, or rather when, they come here, we have to be just as welcoming as we were to Major Carrigan. Hopefully, I can trade with them too, and they don't just come in and take all our horses."

Harriet looked out the window at the Bee across the road. "What about the store?" she asked.

Eli put his arm around her shoulders. "My guess is they won't be buying anything from us. If they see something they need, they'll just take it. I'm sorry Harri."

"We'll have to close down," she mumbled.

Eli agreed. "Yes, it may come to that, but let's see what happens."

"We can't get any inventory anyway," Harriet sighed. "So there's no point if we don't have anything to sell. We should be buying for fall and winter right now."

Eli wished he could be more reassuring about the days ahead, but he was truly afraid that their lives were about to get much worse. "Try to be patient Harri, and hope that the Union fully secures

Knoxville in a couple of months. If that happens, things will open up again and supplies can get through. How about getting away for a day and come with me to church in Jonesborough on Sunday? I could use your company on the ride, and the folks over there always want to see you. Please come with me," he pleaded.

Reminded again of what a poor excuse for a preacher's wife she was, Harriet looked away. It terrified her to think they might lose the farm and the store. Then all she would be was the wife of a struggling minister. The idea suffocated her, but she managed a weak smile. "I'll come if you promise not to make me linger for hours," she whispered.

Eli laughed. "We'll start home right after lunch. I promise, Harri."

---

30

Sunday June 13, 1863
A good day. The folks in Jonesborough are holding up even though most businesses have been shut down and the courthouse is boarded up. People are sharing food. Most of the livestock has been taken. Despite all, they're trying to stay positive, holding prayer meetings most evenings. Lots of questions and opinions about the Johnsons and the attack on Rice and Lelia. Hopeful talk about the assembling of Union troops and movement towards Knoxville. Harri was wonderful today—no hint of how much she hates helping me with the church work. Rice is taking some horses to the Union tomorrow. Stay away Devil and don't start any trouble.

Early Monday morning, Rice and Ford rode up the ridge trailing two Morgans and two American Saddlebreds. They stopped just at the top to survey the valley below and the woods on the other side of the stream. Ford squinted and shielded his eyes. "I don't see no soldiers. You sure they be there, Mr. Rice?"

Rice nodded. "Pop says they're way back in the woods where you can't see them. Let's take the horses down to the pasture on this side of the stream. You stay with them and I'll ride over to the camp and see if they have any horses for us."

The sentries stepped out of the woods when Rice rode up, asking him the same questions they had put to Eli. "Who are you? What do you want? What makes you think Major Carrigan or Lieutenant Hunt are here?"

Rice tried to keep his voice calm even though he felt his heart skipping and the sweat creeping down his neck and chest. "Look, I know they're expecting me if you'll just let them know I'm here."

Finally one of the sentries agreed to see if anyone would see him and disappeared back into the woods.

"That your slave over there?" the other sentry asked.

Rice shook his head. "No. He's a free man who works for us. We don't keep slaves."

"Uh-huh. I thought all you people down here owned slaves," the sentry sneered, just as Lieutenant Hunt walked out of the woods and glared at him.

"Get back into the woods Corporal," Hunt ordered and turned to Rice. "Thanks for coming. Let's see what you've got."

Rice signaled to Ford to ride over with the horses. Hunt inspected each one. "These will do fine. We don't have any ready to trade over to you today, but if you come back at the end of the week, we'll have some ready to go. Wait here while I get your cash."

Rice tucked the envelope into his shirt when Hunt returned. "Thanks Lieutenant. So should we bring more horses the next time we come or just pick up the ones you want us to stable?"

Hunt rubbed his beard. "Bring more if you can. We have about a dozen more we'd like to change out."

Rice and Ford mounted their horses and turned to leave. "Any word on getting some lumber, Lieutenant?" Rice asked.

Hunt shook his head. "Sorry, no. Maybe in a few weeks."

Not surprised, but still disappointed, Rice waved his hand. "All right then. We'll see you at the end of the week," he said, as he and Ford rode off across the pasture toward the ridge. When they reached the plateau on the slope of the ridge, Rice pulled up and Ford stopped behind him. "What do you think of this spot for a house?" Rice asked.

Ford looked around at the moist green valley. "Pretty nice here, Mr. Rice. Good land for grazin or growin crops. You thinkin of buildin your own place?"

Rice smiled and started riding on up the slope. "Maybe. If things work out, maybe."

At the top of the ridge, they paused behind the rock out-croppings and looked down at the farm and the Bee. "Riders Mr. Rice," Ford whispered and pointed toward the Bee.

Rice shielded his eyes and squinted. "Looks like six or eight at least. This can't be good. It might be the Confederates. Thank God Pop is home today to help Mother through this."

Ford stared at Rice. "She a strong lady your mother. I spect she could scare off pretty much anybody."

Rice smiled, thinking how pleased his mother would be to know what Ford thought of her. "Yes, but Pop is much better at keeping calm and that's surely what we need right now. Let's ride east a ways and down into our far pasture so we'll be out of view."

Backtracking, they stayed below the crest of the ridge and rode about a half-mile before crossing over, well out of view of the barn or store. Here the slope was lower with a grove of trees at the bottom. As they rode back west in the pasture, they found horses lazily grazing. Now and then they stopped to check on one or another, so it would appear that they were just minding the herd. As they got closer to the paddock, they could see the gray glint of uniforms by the gate. Eli was with them and they could hear laughing and friendly conversation. "Ahh—here's my son now," Eli said, motioning to Rice to join them when they rode up. Ford stayed behind to unsaddle their horses and turn them into the paddock. "Rice, this is Colonel Reese Jones. He came all the way over from Greeneville just to have a look at our horses."

Rice extended his hand. "Welcome Colonel Jones."

"I see you've lost an arm son. Where'd you fight?" Jones asked.

Rice shook his head. "I'm sorry to say I never had a right arm sir, so you might say I've been fighting all my life, just not in the War."

"I see," the Colonel said quietly. "Well, you're doing a fine job with these horses. Your father tells me you run the barn operation."

Rice swept his arm around. "Thank you sir, but we all work together here."

"I understand it's your idea to breed Arabians," the Colonel continued. "They're fine horses. We're lucky to have a few of them with us, but we'd surely like to have more."

Keenly aware now that Jones wanted his Arabians, Rice tried to play down their quality. "We're just getting started with them sir, so they're not of the highest standard yet. It's going to take us a few breeding cycles to get them right."

Jones frowned. "I think you are too much of a perfectionist, son. They look very high quality to me, just like most of the rest of your stock. We may be needing some of your herd in the coming weeks. Now that I've seen what you have, I know who to turn to when the time comes. Thank you for showing us around, Reverend," he said shaking Eli's hand. "My boys should have finished filling up the wagon over at the store by now, so we'll be leaving you."

Eli motioned to Rice. "We'll walk over with you Colonel."

"How far did you say the Johnson property is?' Jones asked.

Eli pointed up the road. "A few miles east of here. You

thinking of going there now?"

Jones shook his head. "We don't have time today. Maybe the next time we're over this way. I hear folks think it's cursed or haunted," he chuckled. "What do you think Reverend?"

There was nothing funny at all about the Johnson place for Eli, but he didn't want Jones to know how he felt. "It's a beautiful property, but it's true a lot of people in the community think evil is on the loose over there after what happened. They won't go near it," he said quietly.

The Colonel signaled to his men to mount up. "Well, at least you got the horses out. Until next time Reverend," he said, tipping his hat and then pointing to one of Eli's wagons loaded with items from the Bee. "And by the way, the Confederacy appreciates your contributions to our cause."

Stunned by the towering piles of inventory from the store, Eli couldn't speak and was only able to raise his hand in a weak good-bye. Rice was staring through the store's screen door where he could see his mother sitting on one of the benches with her handkerchief shielding her eyes. Nerva sat next to her holding her hand. Eli pushed past Rice and walked into the store. Bare shelves loomed all around him. A few shoes and pieces of women's clothing were strewn around the floor next to piles of empty boxes. He sank down on the bench next to Harriet and put his arm around her, but words failed him when he felt the sadness wracking her body. They could only stare at the ruin around them and try to take in the idea that they too had become victims of the War.

Rice kicked at the debris on the floor and finally sat on top of the wooden counter, now cleared of all the sweets Harriet had kept there. "They even took the pies and candies," he sighed.

Rice's words seemed to jar Harriet. She stood up, straightened her dress and smoothed her hair into place. "The pies will be stale and full of dust by the time they get to Greeneville," she said in a small, strange voice. "There's nothing more to do here. Thank God

Papa didn't live to see this day," she sighed, as she walked out the door and across the road toward the house.

Eli, Rice and Nerva sat staring at the bare shelves. Their will to get up and do anything draining away. "Nerva, go see after Mrs. Marsh," Eli finally said. "Try to get her to rest for a while."

Without saying a word, Nerva got up and started out the door and then broke into a run. "What's she doing?" Eli asked, turning to Rice, but then he realized that Rice was running too.

"It's Mother. She's fallen down on the porch!" he yelled back.

Later Eli would say that he couldn't remember how he got to Harriet's side. But somehow he did and by then, Rice and Nerva had turned her over onto her back. Her eyes were closed and her mouth gaped open. Blood puddled from a cut on her forehead where she had hit the molding beneath the porch door. Nerva balled up her skirt and pressed it against the cut to stop the bleeding. Rice rubbed her wrists. Eli knelt down and put his ear to her heart and then took one of her hands from Rice and felt for a pulse. The three of them sat there tending to her, urging her back to consciousness, but the minutes passed and Harriet didn't respond. Finally pressing his ear to her chest again, Eli sobbed, "She's gone. Her heart must have given out."

Rice continued to furiously rub her wrists and feel for a pulse. "She can't be gone. She was just here. I don't believe it."

Nerva began wailing loudly and rocking back and forth. Her shrieking brought Morgan and Ford running from the barn. "Be quiet all of you, so I can hear better," Rice yelled. But there was no sound to hear from Harriet. As they stared at her and waited, her very stillness convinced them that she had gone elsewhere.

"Let's carry her inside," Eli said at last.

———

31

July 7, 1863

It's been more than three weeks since Harri left us. But I see her everywhere and she talks to me constantly. All these years I've been comforting people when they've lost loved ones, but I had no idea how strong the spiritual connection with the dead is until now. I should've been telling them to listen for the voice from the other side. Everyone has been very kind and helpful, but it's Harri's presence that keeps me going. I've taken a leave of absence from the churches. I don't seem to have the energy to write sermons or ride to the services. Today is the first day I've written a word. I realize now that I don't understand God at all. The only thing that seems certain is the War around us and our treacherous horse trading of course. Rice is on his way to the Union camp now with more horses.

"How's your father doing?" Major Carrigan asked, while he and Rice were waiting for Ford to bring four horses over to the camp from the pasture.

Rice shook his head. "It's hard. He and my mother were very close. I see him looking like he sees her and then talking quietly. I've even looked myself once or twice to see if she's there, but she's not showing herself to me."

"He's still in shock. It'll get better over time, but he needs to stay busy," Carrigan said. "What about the Confederates—have they been back for horses yet?"

Rice shook his head. "There's so much anti-Confederate feeling circulating around ever since they cleaned out Mother's store and then she died. Most folks—even those siding with them—think they went too far. They might as well have put a bullet in her heart, because their actions killed her plain and simple," he said bitterly. "Anyway they haven't been back for the horses yet."

Carrigan stayed quiet, thinking about how his men often took what they needed from innocent people. Ransacking, pillaging, and confiscating supplies and livestock, especially horses, were common practices by occupying armies. How else could they survive a long campaign? This little trading arrangement with the Marshes was going on only because it suited his army's needs while they prepared for Knoxville. "You know when they come back, it won't be to buy your horses," he warned. "Especially now that we beat them back so badly at Gettysburg."

Rice nodded. "That's what we're expecting. So I've been thinking maybe we ought to finish our trading as soon as we can, Major. The first horses you brought over are in pretty good shape now, so I'd like to return them to you. By my count, you need about six or eight more of ours. Is that about right?"

"Lieutenant Hunt is keeping track of the count, but that sounds right. Plus we need mules," Carrigan said, as he walked with Rice and Ford to the edge of the stream.

"All right then. We'll be back in a few days," Rice said and waved good-bye.

After they crossed the stream, Ford looked over at Rice. "We don't have hardly no mules. The Confederates hitched the best team to the wagon when they took everthin."

"We'll sell them whatever we can," Rice said. "I'd rather they got them and not those other bastards."

Seeing the dark threatening scowl on Rice's face, Ford mumbled, "Yah sir," and kept quiet for the rest of the ride.

This time, when they looked down at the farm from the top of the ridge, all was peaceful and quiet. "Good—no visitors," Rice said, as they rode down the slope into the pasture where the horses were grazing.

"Has Pop been over this morning?" Rice asked Morgan at the barn.

Morgan nodded. "He came over earlier and watched the horses for a bit, but he's gone back to the house now." So Rice hurried toward the house, but turned and crossed the road to the Bee when he noticed the door open. Inside, Eli was sitting on the bench just as he had the day Harriet died.

"Hey Pop. You all right?" he asked, sliding down next to him.

Eli looked around the store. "I can't get used to your mother not being here all the time," he sighed. "Sitting here makes me feel closer to her. She loved running this place."

Rice pushed some trash with his boot. "We should get Nerva to work on cleaning this place up. That way we'll be ready to open up again as soon as supplies start moving."

Eli looked down. "Maybe, but who's going to run it?"

"We could all help out," Rice said quietly. "And once Lelia and I are married, she might like it too. I've been kinda wondering what she'd do all day over here."

Eli looked up and smiled at Rice. "I appreciate you postponing your talk with John Patton because of your mother. But she would want you and Lelia to go ahead and start your life together. You should go see him."

"Thanks Pop. I'd like to go over there this afternoon. I haven't seen Lelia since Mother's funeral. You'll be okay here?" he asked.

Eli stood up and walked toward the door. "I'll be fine. You go ahead. How'd the trading go this morning?" he asked, as they walked over to the house.

Rice described his meeting with Major Carrigan and their decision to speed things up and finish as soon as possible. "How many more trips do you figure?" Eli asked.

"Maybe three or four more, plus we've got to return their horses and whatever mules we can spare," Rice said.

Eli was pleased to hear this news. "Good—it sounds like they're planning to move on soon."

Rice glanced at his father. "They're worried that the Confederates are going to swoop in on us and take all our horses."

"Me too. I'm expecting that to happen at any time," Eli said, his voice flat and tired. "Let's see what Nerva's made for lunch, so you can get over to the Pattons'.

———

*32*

Riding to the Pattons', Rice felt happy for the first time in weeks. His father wanted Lelia and him to go ahead with the wedding. His grandmother's diamond ring was tucked deep in his pocket and he couldn't wait to slip it onto Lelia's finger. Even the dread of asking John Patton for his permission couldn't spoil his mood. But midway up the long drive to the house, he saw a group of gray uniforms riding toward him and he felt a twinge of fear. He rode over to the side of the drive and pulled up to let them pass, but instead they stopped in front of him.

"Rice Marsh, is that you? What are you doing here?" Colonel Reese Jones called out.

"Afternoon, Colonel. I'm visiting the Pattons this afternoon," Rice answered, making sure not to mention Lelia. "They've been very kind to us since my mother passed away."

"Yes, I was sorry to hear that. I'd like to come back and look at your horses again when your father's up to it," the Colonel said.

Hoping to delay the visit as long as possible, Rice looked

directly at the Colonel. "Maybe in a few more weeks. Pop's not seeing anyone just yet."

The Colonel nodded and he and his men started on down the drive. "Be sure to tell him I was asking after him," he called out.

"Weasel," Rice muttered as he watched them ride away. Riding on toward the house, he wondered what Jones had been plotting with John Patton. Maybe they were targeting other Union sympathizers in the community for the Confederates to raid. One thing was certain—he absolutely didn't trust his future father-in-law and there was nothing he could do about it.

Lelia and her mother were quilting together on the front porch, but when Rice rode up, she jumped up and ran out to meet him. Taking his arm, she led him to the house. "I'm so glad you came. It seems like forever since you were here," she beamed.

"You look wonderful," he whispered, thinking how much he had missed her the last few weeks. Reaching the porch, Rice took off his hat. "Good afternoon, Mrs. Patton," he said, nodding to her.

Orpha smiled."It's good to see you here, Rice. How's your father?"

Rice shook his head. "Not so good yet."

"His heart is broken. It's going to take time. We miss him so at the church and hope he'll come back soon," Orpha sighed.

"Yes Mam, I hope so too. Is Mr. Patton here?" he asked.

Lelia giggled. "And I thought you came to see me."

"I did for sure," Rice laughed. "But I just wanted to tell your father something. It won't take long."

"He's in the library. He'll be happy to see you. Lelia will show you," Orpha said.

Inside the front hallway, Rice grabbed Lelia's hand and pulled her close, whispering in her ear, "I've missed you. Wish me luck."

Lelia kissed his cheek, held up her crossed fingers, and then knocked on the library door. "Daddy, Rice is here to see you," she said, stepping away.

"Rice!" John Patton's voice boomed. "Come on in."

Rice stepped into the comfortable wood paneled room, lined with shelves filled with leather bound books, gun racks, fishing rods and deer heads. A gentle cloud of cigar smoke gave the room a ghostly sheen and a welcoming scent all at once. "How's your father?" Patton asked, shaking Rice's hand and then motioning him to sit down across from him.

Rice slid into one of the big leather chairs and immediately felt small and vulnerable. "He's not himself yet sir. Thank you for asking," he managed to say, but his voice sounded too high and far away.

Patton shook his head. "Your mother was a wonderful woman— such a loss for all of us."

"Thank you," Rice said clearing his throat. "Sir there's something I want to talk to you about."

"I suppose you saw Colonel Jones leaving, and you're wondering what he was doing here," Patton said.

Rice shifted uneasily in his chair. "Well yes, I was wondering, especially after what he did to my mother over at the Bee, but actually I came over to ask you about something else."

Patton stared at Rice. "What is it son?"

Rice breathed in deeply. "Sir, Lelia and I want to get married. I'm asking your permission."

Patton jumped up and towered over Rice. "You two have already talked about this?"

Rice stood up too and met Patton's stare. "We have sir, but it's important to us that you approve."

Patton paced around the room smoking his cigar. Just as Rice was thinking that he was going to refuse, he stood very close to him and put his hand on Rice's shoulder. "Our views about this War and the Confederacy are quite different I suspect. That could be a big problem for you very soon," he said, pausing. "But I also know Lelia has been attracted to you most of her life, and you seem to care deeply for her. Maybe that will be enough to carry you two through the changes and hard times which will surely come when the War is over and the Confederacy succeeds over the Union."

A surprising calmness settled over Rice. He knew now that Patton approved of the marriage and was just using this moment to needle him about his views on the War. "I love Lelia, sir and nothing is going to change that. Whatever happens with the Confederacy, I will take care of her and I won't let it come between us. We are looking to the future, not the past or even what's happening out there right now."

Patton smiled and shook Rice's hand. "You're very wise and strong. I hope you and Lelia will have a happy long life together."

"Thank you sir," Rice stammered.

Patton laughed and clapped him on the back. "Let's go find Mrs. Patton and our girl."

Of course the Burkhart diamond ring was too big for Lelia's dainty finger, but she loved it just the same. "I'll wear it around my neck for now," she laughed. "Until I can wrap some silk around the band to hold it in place on my finger."

"When do you want to get married?" Rice asked, as she walked him down the drive when he was leaving.

"Soon," she answered quickly. "I don't want anything else to happen that might get in our way."

Rice breathed a big sigh of relief. "I'm glad you feel that way. Something is surely going on with the troops around here. There's talk that the Union is going to try to drive the Confederates away from Knoxville for good."

Lelia nodded and pursed her lips. "I know. I think that's what Colonel Jones was talking to Daddy about today."

Rice stopped walking and put his arm around Lelia. "Could you be ready by August 15th?" he asked, hoping that he would have all the horse trading with the Union settled by then.

Lelia searched his face, wondering why he had chosen that date. "Mama will have a fit, but yes, I can be ready."

"All right then—I'll talk to Pop about marrying us." Then

thinking of Eli, he added, "I need to get going. Things are still rough at the house without Mother." He pulled her close and kissed her deeply, feeling the old heat sweeping over them. Pulling back, he said, "How about we just get married tomorrow!" he laughed, as he climbed into the saddle.

Lelia laughed too and slapped his leg. "Honestly Rice—get out of here, but come back as soon as you can," she said, blowing him a kiss.

———

## 33

As it turned out, it was weeks before Rice rode back to the Pattons' property. Every few days, he and Ford made the trading trips to the Union camp. By the end of July, they were able to return all but two of the army horses in healthy condition, and they were getting close to filling the request for twelve more Morgans, Tennessee Walkers and American Saddlebreds. Although they still had a large number of horses on the farm, they had traded out most of Mack Johnson's stock. Rice worried that if Colonel Jones came by, he would surely notice the number of horses missing. How would he and Pop explain that?

In a way, even though they grieved for Harriet, life had taken on a new rhythm without her guiding hand. Despite the constant worry over completing their Union arrangement and their anxiety about the Confederates showing up to seize their land and horses, the members of the Marsh household went about their daily tasks of keeping the farm running. Eli visited the barn daily, but mostly spent his time helping Nerva harvest vegetables and fruit. She was very good in the kitchen, canning and preserving almost daily. When there was time, she and Eli worked on cleaning up the Bee. Neighbors dropped by from time to time when they needed supplies, but it was rare that Eli had what they needed. Everyone pleaded with Eli to keep the Bee going and they worried him about when he would be getting back to the church. But all he would say about being a minister was that he was looking forward to marrying Rice and Lelia. Rice was holding on to the hope that the wedding would not just be a celebration for him and Lelia, but maybe a turning point in his father's grieving as well.

*August 1, 1863*

*Two weeks until Rice's wedding—are you going to be there Harri? Orpha and Lelia have been here and at the church several times. They're planning to use some of your flowers to decorate the sanctuary and then there'll be a reception afterwards on the church lawn. I'll be looking for you all day. Tomorrow is Rice's last trading trip to the Union camp. Such a relief to finish this risky business. I know you didn't approve, but it's been a meaningful mission for Rice and he has done a good job. Watch over him Harri.*

The next morning Rice burst into the house causing Eli to rush into the front hallway. "Pop, Pop, they're gone—Completely gone!" he panted, mopping the sweat from his face and neck and unbuttoning his soaked shirt.

"Thank God," Eli said. "Now we can stop all this sneaking around. Are you sure, son?"

"Ford and I looked through the whole campsite in the woods. All you can see are the remains of a few fires. They even raked over the ground to cover footprints. We couldn't even tell for sure which way they went."

Eli stared out the window at the blue mountains. "How much did we lose?"

Rice laughed. "We actually made almost two thousand in cash. They kept their bargain and paid me each time."

Eli shook his head. "Amazing, we managed to profit off this War. It's surely the Devil's work."

"Look at it this way Pop. We can use the money to get the Bee going again after things settle down around here. It'll be a small way of starting over for this whole area."

Eli looked down. The thought of running the Bee without Harriet filled him with sadness, and tears welled up in his eyes. "We'll see," he said quietly.

Rice put his hand on his father's shoulder. "Do you think the Union breaking camp like that means their move on Knoxville is about to happen?"

"I think they're starting to marshal their troops closer that way and Major Carrigan's unit is surely part of it. I bet we could pick up their trail west of here if we needed to," Eli mused.

"I know it was treacherous having them here, Pop, but I liked them. At least we were able to help them out with the horses. I would have done more if they had asked."

Eli smiled. "You did fine, Rice. If you think about it, horses are essential to the armies in this War. They keep everything moving— carrying troops, generals, secret communications and pulling heavy loads of supplies, guns, canons and wounded soldiers. Their quiet strength and bravery puts most men to shame. Without them, it would be a very different fight all together. So yes son, I think you did just fine by the Union."

Eli's sudden, fierce passion for the horses didn't surprise

Rice. "I'm proud of what I did Pop. I'm just saying that I wish I could have done more. Anyway, now we have a lot fewer horses than we did a few weeks ago. I've been trying to think of how to explain that to Colonel Jones if he shows up. I didn't tell you that he was over at the Pattons' the last time I was there."

Eli's face turned dark. "You talked to him?" he growled.

"Not really. I mean he passed me on the drive and asked me what I was doing there and how you were," Rice answered quietly.

Eli paced around the sitting room. "He's up to something, and John Patton is probably in on it too," he seethed. "I hope you and Lelia are able to stay out of that evil nest over there."

"We'll be over here with you, Pop, remember," Rice said, trying to calm Eli down. "Mr. Patton is not going to knowingly put Lelia in danger. So that might help to keep Colonel Jones away from our farm."

Eli frowned. "It's too bad you and Lelia have to start out this way, but maybe someday you'll look back on all of this and see how lucky you were to have had each other and to have made it through."

Nerva tapped on the door. "Y'all can eat when you want. I'm takin' some food over to Ford and Morgan."

"Thank you Nerva. Take your time over there," Eli said, smiling at Rice and then added in a low voice, "She's a survivor and she's thriving on helping us. I think she and Ford want to get married too."

"That would be fine," Rice agreed. "But I hope they stay on here. We need them to keep this place running."

"Maybe now she'll tell us what happened at the Johnsons'," Eli mused.

Rice walked out toward the kitchen. "Maybe now we don't really want to know, Pop," he said, worrying that it would turn out that John Patton had been involved.

---

## 34

Saturday, August 15, 1863

It seemed to Eli that except for the Confederate troops, most of the county turned out for Rice and Lelia's wedding. The crowd of families and friends spilled out of the church and onto the front lawn. Loud cheers and clapping rang out when Eli pronounced them man and wife. Orpha's house staff served heaping trays of food and drinks until late afternoon, and music and laughter drifted through the party. For a few hours the War seemed far away and forgotten. Late in the day, Rice and Lelia climbed into the waiting buggy and started home to the Marsh farm for their first night together. Only then did the crowd let go of the brief euphoria and begin to drift away. Orpha and John Patton and their staff packed up the remains of the party and started the drive home.

Eli closed up the church and as the sun was setting, he walked over to the cemetery to say goodnight to Harriet. He had seen her earlier, standing next to Rice and Lelia during the ceremony and then later moving through the crowd. "Thanks for being there today, Harri. You gave me the strength I needed," he whispered. "I'm going over to your brother Will's house tonight, so the children can have our house all to themselves. They don't need us prowling around at home like we do most nights. Nerva said she'd make dinner for them and then stay at the barn tonight." He reached down and patted her headstone. "It'll be dark soon. I'll see you later."

"We're home, Mrs. Marsh," Rice laughed, when they pulled up to the house and he leaned over and kissed her.

"Quick let's go inside and lock the doors," Lelia said, as Rice helped her out of the buggy.

Inside, Lelia took off her veil and shook out her hair, while Rice brought in her bags and then took the horse and buggy up to the barn. The house was quiet and cool with the evening breeze ruffling through the curtains. She walked quietly through the rooms, running her fingers over Harriet's things—elegant English china, framed pictures, rose patterned lamps, delicate crocheted doilies, intricately embroidered pillows, and highly polished mahogany tables and chairs. Just like her own mother, everything was a reminder of a beautiful, refined woman permanently captured in a rural, agrarian setting. Lelia wished she had known her better.

"Do you think you can be happy here for the time being?" Rice asked, when he came in.

"I'm certainly going to try," Lelia whispered, kissing him lightly. "But it's a little unnerving being here with your mother so recently gone, and yet so much of her still here," she said, sweeping her hands around the room.

"I know, honey," Rice said sadly. "But she'd be very happy about today and that you are here with me now at last and for the rest of our lives.

Lelia took his face in both of her hands. "Let's go upstairs. Everything's going to be fine."

Upstairs, Rice led her to his room which Nerva had transformed into a bridal suite with crisp fresh linens and bouquets of flowers. Candles glowed softly in crystal hurricane lamps, giving the room a magical feel. Rice smiled when he saw the delight on Lelia's face. "You go ahead and change. I'm going to lock up and turn down the lamps downstairs. I'll be right back," he said, closing the door behind him and hurrying down the stairs. After he bolted the doors and turned the kerosene lamps low, he went to the kitchen and pulled towels over the food Nerva had set out for them. They were both too excited to eat just now, but it was possible they might be hungry later on.

As he started back up the stairs, a rustling sound in the sitting room made him turn around. Thinking he hadn't closed the windows enough, he crossed the hallway to check again. Just out of the corner of his eye, he saw a shadow move away from the door to the side porch. Standing completely still and not breathing, he waited to see if someone would pass the windows on the front porch, but no movement or sound came. "What the Devil," he murmured as he turned the knob on the side porch door which was firmly latched. Had he imagined both the sound and the shadow he wondered as he went around checking all the doors and windows again. Then he realized he hadn't looked at the window in Eli's study because the door was closed. Opening the door to the dark little room, he could feel a breeze coming through the half open window. As he was pulling it down and latching it, Lelia's soft voice cut through the quiet making him jump.

"You coming up, honey?" she called.

"Be right there," he answered and hurried to the hallway, where he found Lelia, wrapped in a lace robe, halfway down the stairs. "Sorry that took so long," he said, trying to sound casual, as he joined her on the stairs. Casting one more look into the dimly lit sitting room and the porch beyond, he saw nothing unusual. "You look gorgeous Mrs. Marsh," he whispered, holding her tightly as they went back to his room and closed the door. He undressed quickly and slid under the covers into her waiting arms. For the rest of the night, they were totally absorbed in each other, and if there were any more mysterious noises or roaming shadows, they were completely unaware. The next morning they woke to the sun streaming through the windows and the early morning sounds of the horses galloping into the pastures.

"I'm going to check on things over at the barn," Rice said softly, running his finger down Lelia's back. "After breakfast, let's take a ride and I'll show you around the farm."

Lelia yawned. "You go ahead. It takes me a little while to get started in the morning. I'll see you downstairs."

Rice kissed her and smoothed her hair back from her face. "I still can't believe you're here," he laughed, as he pulled on his clothes. "Take your time. I'll see you in a little while."

In the kitchen, he found Nerva making biscuits. She handed him a cup of coffee. "How was the wedding Mr. Rice?"

Rice smiled. "Wonderful and thank you for making the room upstairs so nice for us. Lelia will be down in a bit and then we'll have breakfast. I'm going to the barn first." As soon as he was outside, he remembered the shadow from the night before. So he walked around the porch from the front to the back, but found nothing out of place and the glass doors to the sitting room were still bolted from the inside. So who or what had he seen he wondered. He needed Eli to come home and check his study. Maybe he could tell if someone had been in there.

Morgan and Ford had all the barn maintenance under control and there were no problems with any of the horses. They assured Rice that they could get along without him for another day while he showed Lelia around the farm. As Rice was going back to the house, Eli rode in. "Hey Pop—Lelia and I are about to have breakfast. Come join us."

Eli smiled. "I've already eaten, but I'll have some coffee. Everything all right here, son?"

Rice's face turned red. "It's fine. Thank you for letting us have the house to ourselves last night."

Eli waved his hand. "You two need time alone. It's the least I could do."

"Pop, I thought I saw someone on the porch outside the sitting room last night when I was locking up," Rice said, as they walked toward the house.

Eli frowned. "You couldn't tell who it was?"

"It was just a shadow. So I checked the whole house again and I found the window in your study was half open. Everything looked okay to me, but someone might have been in there."

"Confound it," Eli growled. "Why can't they just leave us alone? Nothing frightening ever happened around here, until all these strangers on the loose from the armies started roaming around harming good folks in their own homes."

"Look Pop, we don't know who it was, and to tell the truth I couldn't find anything out of order this morning. Maybe you'll notice something in your study," Rice said, trying to calm Eli down. "Anyway I didn't say anything to Lelia about it. Can we just keep it that way unless there's a reason to tell her?"

Eli nodded. "Absolutely. There's no reason to upset her on her first full day here."

Lelia opened the front door for them when they walked up, and Eli kissed her on the cheek. "Welcome home," he said putting his arm around her shoulders.

"Thank you. I love being here," she said, smiling and taking Rice's hand. "Nerva set breakfast in the dining room for us."

Eli chuckled. "Well now that's special. I'm sure your Mother approves," he said, winking at Rice. "You're already brightening things up around here for us Lelia," he added as they sat down.

After a leisurely breakfast, Rice and Lelia left for their ride around the farm, and Eli hurried to his study. Right away he saw that the papers on his desk were not as he had left them and his

Bible was turned upside down which he would never do. As he sat down behind his desk, he noticed one of the lower drawers was ajar. Clearly someone had been in there after he left for the wedding the day before. Opening the window, he found the screen unhooked at the bottom, but still hanging on the hinges. A small or medium sized person could have slipped in or out without removing the screen. The idea that an intruder had been in the house endangering Rice and Lelia was very unnerving. Eli went back into the hallway, unlocked the back porch door and stepped out. Nothing at all was out of place. He walked the length of the side porch past the parlor doors where Rice had seen the shadow and on around to the front porch. Again he could find nothing wrong. What had this person been looking for in his study he wondered.

Obviously, whoever it was knew that no one, except maybe Nerva, was in the house and he wasn't expecting Rice and Lelia to return home early that evening he reasoned. Surprised by the couple, he got out quickly, but not away before Rice came back downstairs. Eli went back to his study and looked through his desk. Nothing at all seemed to be missing. But that wasn't too surprising. The only papers he kept there were related to the churches he served, cemetery records, dates of burials, marriages, baptisms, and hundreds of sermons cataloged by topic and date. He never kept cash there. He and Harriet had always kept their savings, important personal papers and Harriet's small cache of Burkhart jewelry in what they called the heart of the house. That was actually a small stone hole in the basement next to the base of one of the chimneys. It was covered by similar chimney rock, making it undetectable to anyone, but those who knew it was there. He would check the heart later, but felt certain he would find it undisturbed.

Turning to the bookcases behind his desk, he noted all his favorite books were there, as well as all the diaries he had written over the years. Staring at those bound journals, he suddenly shivered and jumped up to check his day jacket which he always wore in the house. It was hanging on the peg on the back of the door as usual, but when he reached into the inside breast pocket, he moaned. Frantically he checked all the other pockets and then sat down stunned. GONE! His diary with all his recent personal entries over the last two months. It included what he knew about the Johnsons, and even worse about his horse trading arrangement with the Union and the location of their camp on the Marsh property. Feeling weak with despair, he sank down to the floor, crying out, "GOD HELP US HARRI. THEY KNOW! WE'RE FINISHED NOW!"

———

# 35

Lelia shielded her eyes against the sun, when she and Rice reached the top of the ridge and stared down at the valley below. "I had no idea your farm went so far back," she said, reaching her hand out to him.

"It's beautiful here isn't it? It's my favorite part of the farm," Rice said, squeezing her hand and then leading the way down the path to the land that jutted out from the hillside, before dropping again. "What do you think about this spot for our house?" he asked, sweeping his arm wide.

Lelia took a long look all around. "It is so beautiful here, but it's sort of far from the road, isn't it? I mean how will we move things in and out of here. Is there another way out to the main road that I can't see?" she asked, frowning.

Disappointed, Rice didn't answer right away. "I guess that's why I like it so much. It's a secret valley in here and no one would bother us," he said, looking at her sideways.

"So there isn't another way in or out?" she asked again.

"There's no road, but you can cut through the woods over there and hit the road to Jonesborough. We go that way sometimes," he explained.

"Well, maybe we could make a road in from there," she suggested.

"Maybe so, after the War's over," Rice answered, dejected that Lelia had pointed out a big problem with his dream home. "Come on let's find a place along the stream for lunch," he said, starting down the slope again.

Under a grove of trees by the stream, they stopped and watered the horses and then tethered them to one of the trees. After lunch they lay on the blanket looking up at the sun shimmering through the leafy maples. Lelia reached in her pocket and handed Rice a small wrapped box. "Something to remember our wedding by," she whispered softly.

Rice pulled off the paper. Inside the box was a gold filigree pocket watch on a chain. Rice whistled and opened the case. A picture of Lelia in her wedding dress glowed inside the cover opposite the creamy Roman numeral watch face. The back cover was engraved with the date August 15, 1863. He leaned over and kissed her. "It's magnificent. I'll keep it with me always," he said, pulling her up off the blanket. "Let's start back."

This time they rode along the base of the ridge until they reached the lowest slope on the east end of the farm. Rice pointed to the thick woods. "There are several acres of trees here, Lelia, but like I said before, when you get to the other side you're on the road to Jonesborough."

"So if we built a house back up there on the plateau, you could make a road through these woods?" Lelia asked.

"It'd be a hard job, but it could be done," Rice agreed, turning his horse to cross over the slope to the pasture on the other side. "It's just something to think about, honey. We don't have to decide anything now. Even if the War ended tomorrow, it would probably take a year to get enough materials together to build a road, not to mention a house."

"It'll be fun planning a new house," Lelia laughed. "But right now, let's race back to the barn," she called, galloping off ahead of him.

Rice laughed too, watching her race away with her long dark hair flying behind. He didn't try to catch her, but instead just enjoyed the beauty of her gliding along effortlessly in complete union with her horse. When they reached the horses grazing in the pasture near the paddock, they slowed down to a trot and rode into the barn.

Eli was there talking to Ford and Morgan, but he stopped when the couple rode up."Have a good ride?" he asked, smiling at their bright red cheeks and Lelia's wind-blown hair.

"It's beautiful land," Lelia said, smoothing her hair. "I had no idea it's such a big farm."

Eli smiled. "Not too many folks even know about our valley on the other side of the ridge, and we sort of like it that way. Say, would you mind if I borrow Rice for a little while. We need to talk a little business."

"Not at all. I need to clean up anyway," she said, swinging the picnic basket down from the saddle.

Rice walked her out of the barn. "I'll see you in a bit," he said, kissing her on the cheek.

In the barn, Eli was pacing back and forth in front of the stalls. "What's up Pop?" Rice asked, unbuttoning his shirt to cool off.

"You were right about someone being in my study last night," Eli said quietly.

"I knew I saw someone!" Rice exclaimed, feeling relieved that he hadn't imagined it, but now frightened again at the close call. "Is anything missing?"

"Whoever it was, went through my things without tearing the place to pieces," Eli sighed and slumped down on a bale of hay. "My diary—the one I've been writing in lately is gone."

Rice felt confused. "That's not so bad, Pop. I mean there's so much stuff in our house to take. Why would anyone want your diary?"

"You don't understand, son. I write about everything I think about and do and what goes on here on our farm. Sometimes it's about you and your mother or Morgan and Ford and Nerva, but I also write about other people I meet and talk to and their personal views. Our business arrangement with Major Carrigan has been a running topic lately," Eli stopped and stared at Rice.

Rice's body stiffened. "So, if the person who has your diary has read it, then he knows about the horse trading and the Union camp?"

"That's it," Eli said simply. "But now we have to ask ourselves who would have been looking for my diary or who would see it as something worth stealing?"

"Pop, a lot of people know you like to journal write. I think we're looking for someone who suspected we were doing something with the Johnson horses."

"Like Colonel Reese Jones maybe or one of his cronies," Eli growled. "I've been wondering why he hasn't been back. And don't forget he seems to be close with John Patton who's probably seen me make notes in my diary. He could have told Jones about the timing of the wedding and when the house would be empty."

"Well if it's Jones, then he was just using our horses as an excuse to look at our farm and survey the house," Rice said angrily, kicking at one of the stalls.

"I think we ought to have a talk with John Patton," Eli said quietly. "He's your family now, and I can't believe he would knowingly put Lelia and you at any risk over here."

Rice paced around the barn. "Lelia wants to pick up some more of her things soon. Why don't you ride over there with us, and maybe we can talk to him while she's busy packing up," he suggested.

"Let's do it soon," Eli agreed, as he walked out of the barn. "In the meantime, I've asked Ford and Morgan to start watching the house at night again. We'll need to take turns with them some. I hope Lelia will understand."

"I'll talk to her. She'll be fine. None of this is your fault you know, Pop," Rice said, putting his hand on Eli's shoulder.

Eli walked away, shaking his head. "You're wrong Rice. All of this is because of me and the horses."

———

36

*August 17, 1863*

*I'm expecting the Confederates to accuse me of aiding the enemy. I suppose they'll jail me and probably take our farm and what's left of the store. If they have my last diary, then they know everything, so they may take Rice too. I've told Morgan and Ford they should be prepared to run into the woods with Nerva and not come back. Hopefully they'll let Lelia go back to her folks until Rice is released. I'm sorry Harri. I've made such a mess of our lives.*

Lelia was excited about collecting the rest of her things. She talked continually during the hour's ride about the trunks she had packed with clothes, linens, china, wedding gifts and her favorite books. Her lively chatter and musical laugh made the ride pass quickly and lifted the men's spirits. "This is how it should be isn't it Harri?" Eli said under his breath. "Is it possible that this charming creature's love of life will save us all in the end?"

But their light-hearted mood turned apprehensive when they reached the top of the Patton drive and saw a group of Confederate soldiers and horses congregated on the front lawn. "Daddy must be having a meeting. Hope he has time for us," Lelia said, nudging her horse forward. Rice followed her and Eli came last with the wagon.

The soldiers casually watched them pull up to the house, as Orpha Patton flew down the porch steps and hugged and kissed everyone. "Goodness Mama—I've only been gone two days," Lelia laughed.

Orpha sniffed and dabbed her eyes. "It seems much longer. Come on in. Your Daddy will be so glad you're here. You'll stay for lunch of course," she said, opening the big front door.

In the cool of the parlor, Eli sank down into a wing chair. "I hope we haven't picked a bad time to come, Orpha," he said, motioning toward the soldiers outside.

"Nonsense—you are family!" she exclaimed. "There's never a bad time for you to be here. I'll just let John know, and he'll finish up right away," she added, gliding down the hallway.

"You all make yourselves comfortable," Lelia said. "I'm just going to run upstairs and see if there's anything else I want to pack."

"Take your time," Rice said, smiling as she ran up the curved staircase. "We didn't count on them being here, did we," he murmured, turning to look at Eli.

"Nothing will happen to us here," Eli answered. "Let's see how it goes with John. Maybe he'll give us an escort home, and we'll be all right." And just as he said that, John and Orpha joined them in the parlor along with Colonel Reese Jones and a young captain they didn't recognize. All the men shook hands and Patton introduced the captain as Robert Hollister.

"I understand congratulations are in order," the Colonel said, smiling at Rice. "You're a lucky man."

"I know, sir, thank you," Rice said, looking at John and Orpha.

"And we're so happy to have Rice and Eli as part of our family," Orpha beamed. "I'll get the girls started on lunch," she said. "It was nice to see you again Colonel."

"I guess that's our cue to be going," Jones said, smiling after Orpha. "I'll be back in a few days John. Thanks for your help. And Reverend, I still want to get another look at those horses of yours."

Eli nodded to him. "You're welcome anytime."

Patton walked outside with the Colonel and Captain Hollister and waved them off. Turning back to Eli and Rice, he frowned. "I wish we had known you were coming today."

"Sorry we interrupted you, John. But Rice and I have something to share with you that Lelia doesn't know about yet," Eli said quietly.

Patton frowned. "Is it bad news?"

Rice couldn't wait any longer. In a rush of words, he described seeing someone at the house when he and Lelia got back from the wedding. "He slipped away before I could see who it was. Lelia was upstairs and I didn't want to scare her. I still haven't told her."

"So this someone wasn't after you two and he left as soon as he could?" he asked.

"That's what it seems sir. I think we surprised him."

Eli rubbed his forehead. "The strange thing is, nothing seems to be missing except one of my diaries."

"You mean one of those little black books, you're always making notes in. Who would want that?" Patton asked, looking around the room for a match to light his cigar.

Eli shook his head. "I can't imagine, but I wish them luck trying to read my writing," he chuckled He wondered if Patton already knew what they had just told him. Maybe the search for matches was his way of not looking at them.

"In any case sir, we've started keeping watch at all times. You don't need to worry about Lelia being safe, but we thought you should know what's going on," Rice said.

"Do you need some of my men to help out?" Patton asked.

"Thank you for offering, John, but I think the four of us can handle the watches," Eli said. "But an escort back this afternoon with the wagon full of Lelia's things might be a good idea."

Patton agreed. "Of course, I'll arrange it right away."

"Arrange what Daddy?" Lelia asked, surprising her father from behind with a big hug and kiss on the cheek.

"I've missed you honey," he said, putting his arm around her. "But you are glowing, so life at the Marshes' must agree with you."

Wriggling away from her father, Lelia moved to Rice's side and put her arm through his. "It's the most beautiful land over there, Daddy. Rice took me for a ride around the whole place. It just goes on and on, and there's a secret valley I never knew even existed that's simply magical. You've got to see it. Rice wants to build our house there, don't you honey," she gushed.

Patton stared at Eli and Rice. "A secret valley on your farm—where?"

Rice laughed. "It's not really a secret. You just can't see it from our house or barn. And yes, I would like to build there someday."

"I'd like to see it," Patton said.

Eli smiled. "Sometime when you're over our way, we'll show you. It's really nothing compared to your acreage, John," he said, hoping he could steer away from the talk of a secret place. Thankfully he was saved by Orpha who came in and called them to lunch, where the talk was all about how the wedding went and who was there.

After lunch, two of Patton's hands helped Rice and Eli load the wagon with Lelia's trunks and baskets. Just as they were leaving, Lelia surprised everyone by suggesting to her parents that they come for Sunday dinner after church.

"Are you going to preach Reverend?" Orpha asked.

"I'm going to try," Eli said. "The wedding made me realize how much I need my congregations. Our little Limestone church is a good place for me to begin again.”

"Wonderful news, Eli. We'll be there and for dinner too,” Patton said, extending his hand.

"You sure this won't be too soon?" Orpha asked, putting her arm around Lelia.

Lelia looked at Rice. "We can be ready can't we?"

"Of course. Let's plan on it," Rice agreed.

Eli climbed into the wagon. "We'll look forward to seeing you then," he said, waving and then clicking the reins.

They arrived home late in the afternoon after an uneventful ride back and piled the trunks and baskets in the parlor. Lelia went upstairs to freshen up while Eli and Rice went to the barn with the horses and wagon. "So did you get the sense John Patton already knew about our intruder?" Eli asked, when they were away from the house.

Rice nodded his head. "I thought so, and he might have even already read your diary. He seemed awfully interested in the secret valley talk didn't he?"

Eli frowned. "He and Colonel Jones could have been talking about the diary today. If that's true, I expect we'll see Jones over here before Sunday."

"I'm going to tell Lelia about the other night and explain about the watches. But after she went on and on about our valley being secret, I'm thankful that she has no idea about the horse trading. At least she can't talk about that," Rice said.

"Yes—She's not a risk to us or herself if she doesn't know," Eli sighed as he left the barn. "Ask Ford to bring the horses in a little earlier tonight so he can relieve Morgan on the watch. He's been on it all day."

After a quiet night, Eli rose early the next morning and sent Ford back to the barn to sleep for a few hours. It was mid-morning before Rice and Lelia came down to breakfast. Eli was in his study working on the Sunday sermon when Morgan rushed into the house. "Riders comin!" he called out loudly.

Both Eli and Rice hurried out to the front lawn, just as Colonel Jones and a small unit of soldiers came up the drive. Jones and one of his lieutenants dismounted and walked toward them. "Here we go, Harri," Eli said quietly and looked at Rice.

"Hello Colonel—You here to look at horses?" Eli asked.

Jones shook his head. "Not this morning Reverend. I'd like you and Rice to show me around the Johnson farm."

Eli's heart began to race. "You want to do that now?"

"That's right. Now," Jones said.

Eli spread his hands wide. "Well, I can come, but Rice has a lot of work to do here today. He kinda got behind with the wedding and all."

"I want you both to come," Jones said. "We'll wait here while you get your horses."

Eli turned to Morgan. "Hurry up to the barn and get our horses. You and Ford know what to do around here today while we're gone."

Morgan nodded. "Yessah, we take care of everythin."

"Good morning Colonel," Lelia called from the front porch. "Would you like to come in for some coffee?"

"Thank you Miss Lelia—excuse me—Mrs. Marsh. I don't have time this morning, but maybe another day," he answered, smiling for the first time. Then seeing Morgan coming with the horses, he added, "Gentlemen let's go."

Rice turned to Lelia. "Would you get our hats please," he said, trying not to sound nervous. When she came back out with them, he kissed her on the cheek and whispered, "I love you. We'll be back this afternoon."

Then quietly without a hint of struggle on Tuesday, August 18, 1863, Eli and Rice, surrounded by Confederate soldiers, were taken off their farm. Lelia shielded her eyes from the August sun and smiled and waved as they rode away. Nerva, Ford and Morgan, aware that they might not see Eli and Rice again, watched stone-faced, wondering how long they should wait to run.

———

# 37

Occasionally during the ride, Eli and Rice exchanged glances, but most of the time they were both lost deep in their own thoughts about what might be happening to them. There was no talk at all among the soldiers. As soon as they turned up the drive to the Johnson house, they noticed ominous changes. Confederate sentries saluted the Colonel at the entrance and farther up the hill, large groupings of tents dotted the lawn. The house looked the same from the outside, but Eli shuddered to think of what had happened to Mary's beautiful furnishings. The paddock was filled with horses, and soldiers were cleaning the barn stalls. One rushed over to take the Colonel's horse as the rest of the riders dismounted.

"Let's go down to the barn first," Jones said, motioning to Eli and Rice.

Eli was still taking in the stark changes. "We haven't been here in a couple of months Colonel. Things are certainly different."

"Yes, this property suits our needs," Jones answered. "And of course it was already vacant."

Rice breathed in the smell of sweet hay, thankful the sickening odor of death was gone. "This is the best barn around these parts," he said. "I imagine you could stall all those horses in the paddock in here if you needed to."

"It is grand," Jones agreed, as they passed the stalls leading to the back of the barn.

"Thank God, you got the Black out of here," Eli said, pointing to the stall where the dead horse had been. "That's one we couldn't save."

Reaching the part of the barn, where they had found Mack and Mary's bodies hanging, they were met by a group of local men and some lower level Confederate officers. John Patton was there, as was Sheriff Hawkins. Some were from Eli's congregation and had been at Rice's wedding, but others he had never seen before. Eli and Rice stood very still gazing at the men. "What's going on? Why are we here?" Eli asked, placing his hand over his heart.

Patton stepped forward. "Everything's all right Eli. We just wanted to have a private talk with you and Rice. Here sit down," he said, pointing to two of Mary's Windsor chairs from the house.

As nervous as he was, Eli managed to chuckle. "If you don't mind John, these look like witness chairs. I think Rice and I will stand."

Most of the men laughed at Eli's quick observation and shook their heads. "But it's intolerably hot in here, so water for everyone would be a good idea," Eli added.

Rice stood quietly by his father, impressed by his calmness and ease in this uncomfortable gathering. He, on the other hand, was furious that Lelia's father was part of this occult meeting. He felt trapped and unable to speak and was swallowing rapidly to keep from vomiting. It didn't help that he and Eli were leaning against bales of hay, directly under the beam where Mack and Mary had been hanging. Was this really just coincidence or meant as a cruel warning he wondered.

When the buckets of water were brought in, everyone drank

heavily while mopping their faces and unbuttoning their collars. Despite the airiness of the barn, the late August afternoon humidity hung heavy, and breathing was difficult at best. "So why have you brought us here?" Eli finally asked.

Patton cleared his throat. "Really Eli, just to talk. We have these get togethers from time to time, but we didn't think you and Rice would come unless Colonel Jones escorted you."

"You're probably right," Eli agreed. "We don't get involved in these clandestine meetings."

Colonel Jones held up Eli's diary. "Well you are involved now because of this."

Eli looked at the men surrounding him, most of whom he and Harriet had known their whole life together in Limestone. Who among them he wondered had breached friendship and trust to break into his home and steal his diary? His eyes rested on John Patton. "So I assume John, when we told you yesterday about someone breaking into our house and stealing my diary and putting my son and your daughter, his new bride, in danger, you already knew all about it?"

Patton looked down as did some of the other men. But before he could speak, Rice stepped forward, his anger overcoming his nerves. "Is this true Mr. Patton? How could you be a part of something that might have harmed Lelia?"

"How we got the diary and when is not the issue here gentlemen," Colonel Jones cut in. "You seem to forget that we are at war. Your family business is unimportant. What matters Reverend are your treasonous dealings with the Union, described in your own handwriting."

Rice put his hand on his father's shoulder, as Eli reached into his pocket for his pipe and tobacco. Since they were in the barn, he didn't intend to smoke, but holding it in his hand gave him some comfort. As he filled the pipe with tobacco, he began to talk quietly about the burden his family had faced with taking in the

Johnson horses. "You all know me," he said. "And you know what I love—the church, Harriet and Rice and now Lelia, and then always the horses." He paused and looked around the group. "When the Union soldiers came to the house and asked to buy some horses, I was relieved because we were so overcrowded. I was ready to make a similar arrangement with you, Colonel. So it wasn't about taking sides, which you all know I have refused to do. It was about finding homes and meaningful lives for those superior animals. Rice agreed with me on this. We believed it was an honorable thing to do. But I must admit Colonel that I can't help but feel that because of your actions, I have lost Harriet forever and possibly my faith and the church. So there is some sense of satisfaction that our horses didn't end up with you."

"This is a Confederate state, Reverend. What about allowing the Union to camp on your farm? Was that honorable too?" Jones asked.

"We had no idea they were there," Eli said. "Most of you know our farm, but you haven't been beyond the ridge behind our pasture. There's another valley backed by a stream and woods completely isolated from our house and barn, and it can't be seen from the road. Occasionally I ride through it on my way to one of the other churches because it's shorter than taking the road. Rice wants to build a house over there for Lelia someday. He went over to site the house and noticed the Union camp in the trees. It's surprising that they found that valley, but they did. So I rode over and asked them to leave, and they eventually did a few weeks ago—just disappeared without a trace." Eli sighed and looked around at the faces of his neighbors. All had listened to him in rapt silence, but most looked away or down and could not meet his gaze. "If you know the saying— 'There, but for the grace of God, go I'—then you realize that this could have happened on any of your farms, not just ours. And if you've read my writings, you know that I was certain from the beginning that pure evil has been at work, starting with the murders right here," he said, pointing above his head. Trading the horses just drew us deeper and deeper into the Devil's plot. Losing Harriet and my faith is an unbearable price to pay, and I'll regret it for the rest of my life."

John Patton moved to Eli's side. "Thank you for being so honest with us. We have a few more issues to talk about before leaving. Why don't you and Rice wait up at the house until we're finished."

Colonel Jones escorted them out of the barn and turned them over to two soldiers who walked them up to the house. Eli sank down into one of the rocking chairs which still lined the porch. Rice paced around and peered in the front door. Broken furniture and china littered the floor. Dried clumps of hay and old cigar butts clung to piles of rugs, and tobacco stains oozed on the dulled wood floors and stairs. From what he could see, the dining room table was stacked with maps and charts, and the odor of mold and mildew mixed with rancid sweat and stale smoke burned his nose and eyes. "How can they stand this place?" Rice said in a low voice.

"I doubt it bothers them at all," Eli answered weakly.

Surprised at the change in his father's voice, Rice turned to look at him. "You feel all right, Pop?"

Eli's eyes were closed. "It's just the strain of this day. I'll be fine as soon as we get home," he murmured. But he soon learned that going home was not to be, when Colonel Jones, John Patton and Sheriff Hawkins walked up to the porch.

"Based on what you've written down and now told us, we think it's best you stay here at the camp for a while, Reverend," Jones said. "Your dealings with the Union army make you a threat to our Confederacy. For now you are under house arrest here."

Eli's voice was calm and strong again. "So you're arresting me for making an honest living with my horses during a war?"

"You knew what you were doing was wrong, Eli. You even wrote that trading with the Union was risky business. You're lucky they aren't going to string you up like the Johnsons," Patton observed, shaking his head.

"Sheriff, are you getting this?" Eli asked, not taking his eyes off Patton. "It sounds like the men gathered here today know what happened to Mack and Mary."

"DAMN YOU ELI! WHO DO YOU THINK YOU ARE! NO ONE SAID THAT! ARE YOU ACCUSING ME OF MURDER?" Patton shouted angrily, turning to Hawkins, who stared back, but said nothing.

Rice stepped between his father and Patton. "Am I part of this house arrest too, Colonel?"

"You should be, but no, just your father. You can ride back with Mr. Patton," Jones said. "We'll be watching your place of course. As long as you have no further contact with the Union army, we won't bother you, and your father will be safe. But if you do, you will be arrested, and you won't be seeing your father for a long time."

"So, in a sense I am a hostage too," Rice growled.

Eli stood up. "Go on home Rice. It's important one of us is there to keep the place running. I'll be all right. Maybe I can be of some use here."

"That's very sensible, Eli. Let's get going Rice," Patton said, walking toward the horses.

Rice knew he had to go home to Lelia and the farm, but he felt torn about leaving his father. He worried that Jones would find a reason to move Eli to another camp, and he might never see him again. He stared at his father, making a mental picture, and then nodded his head. "I'll come back in a day or two. Maybe bring you a few things."

Eli nodded and then hugged Rice. "Take Gray home with you. I'll see you soon, you'll see." Sherriff Hawkins stood next to him on the porch, and together they watched as Rice and Patton and most of the other men from the barn rode down the drive.

"I'm sorry about this situation Reverend," Hawkins said. "I feel a bit responsible because I asked you to take the horses to your farm, and then both armies found out about it."

Eli looked at him. "This isn't your fault. I was planning to take the horses anyway. You just gave me approval. What I did afterwards was just business."

Hawkins sighed. "This War has certainly brought the snitches out of the woodwork hasn't it Reverend."

"So it seems," Eli agreed. "I take it you're not going to follow up on Mack and Mary's murders?"

Hawkins looked away. "Reverend, I think we both know what happened here. I'm not going to arrest a whole community of folks right now and open up a rat's nest of raw, bigoted sentiment."

Eli shook his head. "Then the Lord will deal with the guilty and the silent when the time comes, and it will be on their souls forever."

"It's best that way Reverend," Hawkins said frowning. "Remember the saying 'The evil that men do lives after them. The good is oft interred with their souls.' "

"Hmmn—yes—Shakespeare," Eli said, turning into the house. "It's comforting to know you have a literary side too, Sheriff."

Hawkins smiled. "Good luck here, Reverend. I'll try to come back and check on you," he said, as he left the porch for his horse.

Eli waved his hand behind him and went inside. "Look at this place Harri," he whispered, seeing how cruel and complete the wrecking of Mack and Mary's home had been. Anything of value that hadn't been destroyed had been taken away, and the deeper he went into the rooms, the worse the mounting debris and the rotting smell became. And no wonder. Old food and filthy dishes littered the tables and floors. Nerva's room was the same with her clothes and belongings strewn everywhere, but the sickening smell told him that men had been urinating in there instead of using the outhouse or at least going outside. He hurried out the back door and gulped in the fresh air as he stared at the vegetable garden which had been picked clean and then trampled and the chicken coop emptied.

"You still with us, Reverend?" Colonel Jones called.

"Out here, sir," Eli answered and then added, "The air in the house is intolerable. I had to come back here."

"Yes, that's what happens. It won't be fit to live in again. We've made sure of that," Jones said. "You remember Captain Hollister, Reverend. He's in charge of the unit here, and he'll be overseeing you. I have to get back to Greeneville. You're limited to the house and the barn. He'll fill you in on other things," he said, turning to leave.

"I understand Colonel," Eli said, shaking hands with the younger officer.

"Follow the rules, Reverend, and we'll get along fine," Hollister said. "Dinner is around six. We'll talk then."

"Where should I stay?" Eli asked.

"I'm sleeping in the room at the top of the stairs. You can choose any of the others," he answered, walking back into the house.

"Thank you," Eli said to the empty air.

———

## 38

Rice and John Patton parted company before reaching the Marsh farm. "I'd rather you didn't come in just now, sir," Rice said, when Patton suggested stopping by to see Lelia. "I'm going to have to explain to her what's happened to my father. I don't want you there for that. This is between Lelia and me."

"She's still my daughter, but I'll do as you ask this time," Patton snapped, urging his horse on toward home.

Lelia and Nerva ran out of the house to meet Rice when he turned up the drive. Ford stood on the porch with a rifle, and Morgan hurried over from the barn. "Everything all right here?" Rice called out.

"Been quiet all day," Morgan answered.

Lelia kissed him on the cheek. "I've been so worried. Thank goodness you're back. Where's your father?"

Rice took a deep breath. "He's under house arrest over at the Johnsons' for now. You should see that place. It's become a full-blown Confederate headquarters," he said, shaking his head.

Morgan, Ford and Nerva all looked at one another, but said

nothing. Lelia gripped Rice's arm and gasped, "Why? Why would they arrest your father?"

Rice put his arm around her. "It's complicated honey, but the short explanation is that Pop and I did some horse trading with the Union army a while back. Then without our knowing it, they set up a camp on our land over in the woods across from where I want to build our house. Colonel Jones and some others just found out about everything and now they've decided Pop is a threat to the Confederacy." Turning to the others, he added, "I know my father told you to run and hide if anything like this happened. Thank you for staying here with Lelia today. It's a great comfort."

"Truth to tell Mr. Rice, we wuz gonna go in the mornin if you didn come back today," Morgan said.

Lelia's face turned pale. "You were going to leave me here alone? I don't believe it," she said weakly.

"It would never have come to that, Lelia," Rice said quietly. "If I had been arrested too, your father would have already been here to pick you up."

Lelia looked confused. "And just how would he know to do that?"

Rice lowered his voice. "Can we go inside to talk about this please? We're probably being watched right now. So let's try to act normally."

Shocked and wide-eyed, Lelia looked around, as she followed Rice onto the porch, but then surprised him by very calmly saying, "You must be exhausted. Nerva and I will get dinner ready early while you wash up."

Rice smiled. "Wonderful. Can you handle getting the horses in without me tonight?" Rice asked, turning to Morgan and Ford who nodded their heads and hurried off to the barn. "After dinner come back down here, and we'll sit a while," Rice called after them.

As soon as Lelia had discussed dinner with Nerva, she ran upstairs to find Rice. Closing their bedroom door, she moved behind him while he was standing shirtless at the washstand. Putting her arms around his waist, she kissed his back and shoulders. "We're alone now Rice. Can you answer my question?"

Toweling off, he turned to face her. "Honey, the last thing I want to do is hurt you, but what I'm going to tell you is very upsetting."

She put her hands on his face and stared straight into his eyes. "Tell me."

Rice sat down on the bed and began to describe the threatening meeting in the Johnson barn and about her father and some of their neighbors being there. Then he told her about someone being in the house and stealing his father's diary on their wedding night. "It's obvious to us that your father planned that to happen before you and I got back to the house. Whoever it was didn't get away soon enough, and I thought I saw someone when I was closing up for the night."

"How can you be so sure Daddy did that and why would he want your father's diary?" Lelia asked in a tight voice.

"Remember yesterday when we went to pick up your things and Colonel Jones was there meeting with your father? Well, after the Colonel left we told him about the diary being stolen, and he acted like it was a very odd thing to steal. But after today we know for sure he had already read it and given it to Colonel Jones," Rice said.

Lelia frowned. "I still don't understand Rice. Why would a personal diary be so important?"

Rice took Lelia's hand. "I know this is hard for you to accept, but Pop and I think your father has suspected us all along of being Union supporters, and he's been looking for a way to prove it. He knew about Pop's diary writing, and I think he saw that as a possible way to prove that we were working against the Confederacy. So he got someone to sneak into the house and steal it while we were all at the wedding. Unfortunately for us, his suspicions were right, because Pop had written all about our horse trading arrangement with the Union army and later about their camp being on our land. It was all right there in Pop's own writing. Remember how interested your father was when you raved about our secret valley? I bet he couldn't wait for us to leave so he could get to Jones with the news about the location of the Union camp."

Lelia pulled away from Rice and moved to the windows on the far side of the room, trying to wrap her mind around what he had told her. It was all so unbelievable. She had never thought of her father as a serious Confederate collaborator and certainly not a thief. And now at the same time, she was shocked to learn that both Rice and his father were so heavily involved with the Union. It was obvious they had deliberately kept the horse trading arrangement from her because they were afraid she would tell her father. Tears slid down her cheeks, as she realized that she had been married less than a week, and her new husband didn't trust her at all. How could they build a life together when it was clouded by so much secrecy and suspicion? What if something happened to Reverend Marsh? Rice would hold her father and maybe her responsible forever.

Rice slipped his arm around her waist and kissed her hair. "I'm so sorry about all this Lelia. Pop said all along that secrecy was no way to begin a marriage. We have to get through this together and not let it tear us apart."

Lelia looked up at him, and he wiped her wet cheeks. "You have to trust me from now on Rice," she whispered. "Let's get you something to eat, and then we'll figure out what to do."

"You know we can't leave Pop up there," he said as they walked downstairs. "Anything could happen to him."

"Then we'll have to find a way to get him out," she said firmly.

———

## 39

Just after sunset, Morgan and Ford joined Lelia and Rice on the porch. All believed that they needed to get Eli away from the Confederates as soon as possible. But it was Ford who suggested asking Nerva to help. "She know better than any the rest of us how to sneak in and out of there," he said quietly.

"You're right, of course," Rice agreed. "But she hasn't wanted to talk to us about what happened over there."

Ford stood up. "I gonna fetch her if you don mind. She owe her life to Miz Marsh and the Reverend and you too, Mr. Rice. I know she wants to hep out."

It took some time, but Ford finally coaxed Nerva out to the porch. She held tightly to his arm and sat down warily when Lelia patted the chair next to hers

"Thanks for joining us Nerva," Rice said smiling. "We're sort of having a family discussion here and we want you to be part of it."

Nerva smiled shyly. "Thank you Mr. Rice."

Rice leaned forward in his chair and spoke quietly. "Nerva, we've all agreed that my father is in great danger over there at the Johnsons'. We have to try to get him out of there. Can you tell us how you were able to get away on that terrible day?"

"G'on—tell 'em about the tunnel," Ford urged, taking her hand.

Nerva stared down at the floor and spoke barely above a whisper, as she described how she was down in the root cellar gathering up vegetables for dinner when she heard riders coming to the house and then a lot of heavy boots in the kitchen above. She said she heard Miz Johnson say, "What are y'all doing here?" and then "Why are you doing this?" Then it sounded like they knocked her down and maybe kicked her because she cried out. One of the men said, "Useless abolitionist now," and the others laughed. Through the cracks in the outside basement door, she could see them dragging her down toward the barn.

"It was shameful the way they took her," Nerva sobbed.

Lelia put her arm around her. "Did you see their faces?" she asked.

"No, Mam. Their backs wuz to me, but I could tell they weren't dressed like no soldiers," she answered.

"Sounds like she knew who they were, poor woman," Rice sighed. "So what did you do after that?"

Nerva started to tremble. "I be so scared, Mr. Rice. I dropped everything and ran to the back of the root cellar, pulled the grain sacks away from the wall and tugged open this hatch door and climbed onto the ladder that goes down to the tunnel. I'd never been down there before. Just sometimes helped folks get in when they be on the run. I lit one of the lanterns hanging on the ladder and I tried to pull some of the sacks back over the door as best I could before I closed it." Here she stopped talking and took a deep breath, remembering the suffocating blackness of the tunnel and the terror of being buried alive if she couldn't get out at the other end. The others sat waiting for her to go on.

Finally she was able to describe how she crawled on her hands and knees through the dank narrow passage, pushing the lantern in front of her until she came to a wall of dirt and another ladder. Climbing to the top, she barely had enough strength to push away the boards at the top which were covered with brush and rocks. Clawing her way out of the hole, she found herself in thick, dark woods with no idea where she was. After wandering in the dark for hours, she stumbled out onto the road by accident and eventually found a place to hide by the Bee.

"Do you think you could find that place in the woods where the tunnel ended?" Rice asked.

"Nah sir, I don't know where it is. I don't even know how I got here. I was runnin and fallin and cryin. I think the Lord led me here to you good folks," she whispered.

"My father would certainly agree with that, Nerva, and now we'll be able help him thanks to you and the information about the tunnel," Rice said, standing up and pacing around. He had hoped Nerva could lead them back to the tunnel exit in the woods, and then he could sneak into the Johnson house and get his father out. Since that wasn't possible, he would have to go see Eli and tell him where to look for the tunnel entrance. His father would have to slip away when the time was right. "I think I'll take a ride over there tomorrow and take Pop some clothes and a few things. Hopefully we'll get some time alone, and I can tell him what Nerva said."

"Wonder maybe Mr. Rice, if the soldiers already found the tunnel and sealed it up?" Morgan asked. "What Reverend Marsh gonna do then?"

Rice shook his head. "I don't know, but let's hope that hasn't happened."

"I'm going with you," Lelia said. "It'll seem more natural that we're just taking a ride to check on your father and see how he's doing if we both go."

"Not a good idea," Rice said. "What if they decide we can't

leave? Your father would have a fit that I brought you there."

Lelia smiled. "That's exactly why I'm going. They'll let us leave because of Daddy, if what you say about him is true."

Rice frowned, but realized that Lelia's idea made sense. "All right then, but I still don't like it," he said and turned to Nerva. "Do you think you could draw a little map of how to find the tunnel entrance in the root cellar? Pop's already been down there, but he didn't see it."

Nerva smiled. "I'm pretty good at drawin."

Rice smiled at her too. "I think we should all try to get some sleep. Morgan, I want you to ride with Lelia and me tomorrow, and Ford, you and Nerva will have to take care of things here. "See you all in the morning," he said taking Lelia's hand, and thinking how quickly he had temporarily become the head of the Marsh family.

———

40

The rain and wind started after midnight. Rice and Lelia rushed around the house closing all the windows, but not before Harriet's lace curtains were soaked through and puddling everywhere. Taking a lantern, Rice trudged up the muddy drive to the paddock and barn. Little rivers of rain water rushed towards him, sloshing over the tops of his boots. He could just make out the shapes of Ford and Morgan trying to lead the horses from the paddock to the barn. Thank goodness this didn't happen a few weeks ago when we had so many more horses he thought to himself. After a struggle, they were able to secure all the animals in the crowded barn, with some needing to be tied outside stalls in the long aisle—miserable conditions, but better than risking them being overwhelmed and panicked in the paddock.

Rice mopped his face with his handkerchief. "Try to get a little more sleep fellows. I'd still like to leave early tomorrow for the Johnsons'."

Slipping and sliding on what was once the barn drive, he

made it back down to the house. Lelia met him on the porch with towels. "I've never seen a storm like this," he said. "If this keeps up all the roads and bridges will be washed out. We may not be able to get to Pop for days."

"All those poor soldiers out there huddled up in those soaked tents," Lelia said, looking at the rain. "At least your father is inside the house and dry."

Rice sighed. "I hope so, but who knows what's going on over there now."

Eli had sensed the storm brewing earlier in the evening. The heavy dampness riding on the low gray clouds and the leaves turning over in a sultry wind. Ahead of the rumbling thunder, he had mentioned the coming rain at dinner to Captain Hollister who seemed uninterested. Of course, that all changed when the torrential rain started and the wind tore into the sea of tents, sending them flying. Most of the soldiers abandoned their stark belongings and squatted in groups in the house, on the porch, and even in the barn among the horses. Eli was pressed into service, first finding blankets and towels—anything dry, and then shuttling coffee and tea to the men. He was glad to be doing something useful and to offer some comfort. Most of these soldiers were young boys who had never been away from home. They were nervous and frightened by the storm's fierceness.

"I didn't know it stormed like this up here in the mountains, Reverend," one young soldier said. "Do you think God is mad at us?"

Eli smiled and patted the boy's shoulder. "It happens sometimes, but it doesn't usually last that long. I like to look at it as the Lord's way of cleansing the earth now and then."

"So you don't think he's punishing us for the war?" the boy persisted.

Eli thought for a moment. "I'm just a country preacher son. I try to help folks believe in a loving God. I don't believe he punishes people with storms or sickness for fighting for what they believe in. And don't forget it's raining on the Union soldiers too if they're anywhere around here," he said, chuckling as he walked back to the kitchen.

But two days later, Eli had to admit he had been wrong about the length of the storm. Although the wind had calmed, heavy rain continued to fall, and standing water and knee-deep, red clay mud covered the farm and pooled in the barn. When he went up to bed that night, he pulled out some loose writing paper he had found downstairs so he could put down his thoughts.

*August 21, 1863*

*Conditions here are worsening by the minute. The air in both the house and the barn is filled with the stench of human waste and rotten food and water. It's reminding me of that horrifying day Rice and I found Mack and Mary. Both men and horses are so desperately crowded, sickness will surely set in soon if this rain keeps up. Some of the soldiers are already coughing and vomiting. I wonder if these horrible conditions and the threat of serious illness will convince Colonel Jones to move this unit out of here. What will that mean for me? I need to get away, but it seems impossible. Maybe I could slip away during the cleanup, but I don't hold out much hope.*

He tucked the loose pages deep into his inside pocket and stretched out on one of the small beds that had belonged to the twins. His back and legs ached from standing most of the day, but otherwise he didn't feel ill. He drifted off to sleep, feeling Harriet lying beside him. Her sweet rose water smell enveloped him and her hair tickled his nose and made him smile. "I'm glad you're here Harri," he whispered. "I knew you'd find me."

The rain stopped overnight, and a misty sun streamed through the window the next morning. Except for the rose water scent, there was no sign of Harriet, but the calmness Eli felt told him she had been with him through the night. Despite his precarious situation, he felt at peace as he went downstairs to the kitchen.

———

*41*

August 24, 1863

It took two more days for the water and mud to recede and the earth to begin to dry. The roads had become nothing more than deep gullies and boulders, and the bridges had washed away. Still, Rice, Lelia and Morgan set off early in the morning for the Johnson farm. Nerva had drawn a clean diagram of the root cellar with the tunnel entrance clearly marked, but she was still unable to describe where the exit in the woods was located. Rice hoped that Eli might have an idea where the exit might be and how far from the farm it was.

Because the roads were so treacherous, the ride to the Johnsons took more than three hours. The drive to the house had disappeared completely into a steep bank of mud and rocks, littered with remnants of tents and debris from the soldiers. Carrying a satchel with Eli's clothes, his bible, a blank journal and pencil, and a basket of food, Rice and Lelia decided to leave the horses with Morgan down below and try to climb up to the house. When they finally reached the top of the hill, they were covered in mud and leaves, but happy to see that the house was intact and buzzing with activity. Soldiers were rushing about saddling horses and loading wagons. No one seemed to notice them watching, until a voice from behind asked, "What y'all doin here?"

Turning around, they found a mud covered soldier pointing a rifle at their chests. "I'm Rice Marsh and this is my wife Lelia. We've come to check on my father and bring him a few clothes and things. He's staying here," Rice explained

The soldier lowered his gun. "You must mean the Reverend. He's at the house takin care of the sick ones," he said, pointing toward the porch.

"What's wrong with them?" Lelia asked.

"They got some kinda fever and vomitin," he answered. "Started during the storm."

Rice nodded. "Thank you, we'll find him."

"You'll have to ask Captain Hollister if you can see him," the soldier called after them. "And he's gonna want to see what's in those," he added, pointing to the satchel and the basket.

"We understand," Rice said walking toward the house and urging Lelia, "Hurry honey, they look like they're leaving."

Eli saw them coming, and when they got to the steps, he called to them, "Don't come any closer. There's a terrible sickness up here."

Rice smiled up at his father. "It's nice to see you too, Pop. It was no trouble at all coming over here this morning to check on you."

Lelia laughed softly, making Eli smile. It pleased him that Rice and Lelia had the capacity to find humor in the midst of such misery. In fact they were an uplifting sight—so young and energetic and covered in mud from head to toe. "I'm awful glad to see you. I just don't want you to catch this sickness," he said.

"Pop, ask them if you can come down and talk to us. We've brought you some clothes and things, and Lelia's got a basket of food," Rice said.

Eli disappeared into the house to check, while Rice and Lelia sat down on the steps. "Their horses are in terrible shape," Rice said squinting at the bedraggled animals being hitched to wagons. "They were probably crammed into the barn during the storm and they haven't had a chance to exercise and get their strength back."

"It breaks my heart to see them like this. They'll be dead from exhaustion before they get to wherever they're going," Lelia whispered.

"And they'll be better off," Rice said grimly, turning to see Eli and a Confederate officer and aide coming down the steps.

"This is Captain Hollister, my host, so to speak," Eli said, introducing Rice and Lelia.

"I remember meeting you at the Pattons' house. Thank you for letting us see my father. We brought some things for him," Rice said holding up the satchel and basket.

The Captain motioned to his aide to look through them. "You can sit here and talk to your father for a few minutes, but then you'll have to leave. We don't have time to entertain visitors. You'll be watched all the time, so don't do anything foolish," he said, walking away from them.

The aide quickly rummaged through the satchel and basket. "Everything looks okay in there sir," he said, handing them to Eli.

"How's everything at home?" Eli asked, sitting down on the steps.

"The farm is a mess, but the horses are okay. It'll take us a while to get cleaned up," Rice said.

"And the roads and bridges are gone, "Lelia added. "It took us three hours just to get here."

Eli sighed. "Well I'm glad you came."

"What's happening here Pop? Are you all right?" Rice asked.

Eli took out his pipe and filled it with tobacco. "I'm getting by. They're keeping me busy with cooking and taking care of these sick boys. If it hadn't stopped raining, some of them would have surely died by now." Lowering his voice, he added, "They're moving out this afternoon. They got word from Colonel Jones that General Burnside is going to try to retake Knoxville."

"What will happen to you?" Lelia whispered.

Eli looked down. "I don't know. I'm not being treated like a prisoner, but I'm not free to move about much either."

Rice stretched his legs out. "What about inside the house, can you move around on your own in there?"

Eli nodded his head.

"And you can go to the root cellar?" Rice asked, looking away casually.

Eli frowned. "I've been down there a few times. Why?"

Rice glanced over at Eli. "The tunnel is there Pop—at the far end behind some sacks. Nerva has drawn a map for you. The only problem is she doesn't know exactly where the tunnel ends— only that it's in the woods somewhere."

Eli smiled. "So Nerva finally talked. Your mother must be very proud of her progress."

"She did it for you and Mrs. Marsh and all your kindness," Lelia said, taking Eli's hand in hers and pressing a tiny triangle of paper into his palm. "She wanted to help you."

"You've got to get away Pop, before they decide to move you, or worse that you're just too much trouble," Rice warned.

Eli leaned forward. "I'll try this afternoon while they're moving out. You can see how chaotic it's getting already. No one is paying me much mind. You two should be going now. Where are your horses?" he asked, looking around.

"Morgan's got them down below on what's left of the road. There's no drive left to get up here. They're going to have a time getting these wagons out of here," Rice said, standing up to leave. "We'll take a look in the woods at the end of the property here and see if we can find where the tunnel comes out. If we find it, we'll leave you one of our horses."

Eli put his arms around both of them and hugged them tightly. "I'll see you soon at home," he said in a low voice.

Lelia's eyes filled with tears and she couldn't talk, but Rice murmured, "Hurry Pop, we need you," before needing to look away.

Eli watched them walking away hand in hand and then felt Harriet's hand slip into his. "They're going to be all right Harri," he said, and the soldiers watching him looked around, wondering who he was talking to.

"I was startin to think maybe you wasn't comin back," Morgan said, when Rice and Lelia finally made their way back down to the road.

Rice took hold of the horses' reins. "You been all right here?"

Morgan shrugged. "Not many folks on the road yet. One soldier come down here and asked me what I thought I wuz doin. I tole him I wuz waitin on you and he left me be. How the Reverend?"

"He's still all right. Let's get going," Rice said, helping Lelia climb on her horse.

When they reached the woods at the end of the Johnson property, Rice reined in his horse and looked around. "What are we looking for?" Lelia asked.

Rice shook his head. "I don't know, but I figure this must be about where Nerva stumbled out of the woods. So the end of the tunnel must be back in there somewhere. Let's just look around a bit," he said, urging his horse through the dense trees. Lelia and Morgan followed him, but the footing in the woods was a deep swamp of muddy water and snarling undergrowth. Thick clouds of mosquitoes swarmed around them, biting their faces, buzzing into their ears and noses, and attacking the horses. Flailing their arms above their heads, they were forced to turn around and rush back out into the open air on the road.

"What a nightmare," Rice said, coughing and swatting the bugs off his clothes. "I was hoping we could leave a horse for Pop in the woods, but it would be too cruel to tie up an animal in that mess."

Lelia shook the mosquitoes out of her hair and rubbed

the welts on her face and hands. "When your father makes it out through the tunnel, he'll surely be able to find his way home," she gasped. " He knows this area better than anyone, honey."

Rice was still worried. "That's true, but just getting through the tunnel will be hard for him. He's not so young anymore and he'll be traveling in darkness."

"The dark gonna be his friend, Mr. Rice, and he strong. You'll see. When you think he be coming?" Morgan asked.

"Tonight if he's lucky," Rice whispered.

———

# 42

The soldiers spent most of the afternoon shoring up the drive down to the road with boards they had torn off the barn and rails from the big paddock. By late in the day, the unit began to move out and head West. The seriously ill soldiers were to be transferred to Greeneville where doctors were available. Captain Hollister asked Eli to help with preparing them for transport and with outfitting the wagons to carry them. His parting words to him were, "You're to ride to Greeneville with the medical detail. Colonel Jones has plans for you there. You're a good man Reverend. I hope I know you after the War."

Eli spread his hands wide. "I'll pray for you and these good men," he said, as the Captain nodded and rode down the drive to form up on the road.

A young lieutenant came up behind Eli. "You can ride up front with me, Reverend," he said, pointing to the first wagon. "We'll be leaving soon too."

Eli nodded. "I'll just go in and get my things. Maybe use the outhouse, if that's okay with you."

"Go ahead sir, We aren't leaving just yet," the Lieutenant agreed.

Eli hurried up the steps to the empty house. An eerie silence enveloped him as he walked around the first floor, stripped clean of all the military charts and clutter. Only the gooey tobacco stains, mud clods, and piles of dirty rags and garbage were left as reminders. The kitchen was a shamble of broken dishes and rotten food. Certain that no one was around to see, he slipped into Nerva's old room and down the steps to the root cellar. In the dim light he found the back wall that Nerva had drawn and the piled up sacks. Pushing them aside, he saw the small door and pulled it open, revealing the ladder down into the tunnel. Straddling the ladder, he lit one of the lanterns, tugged the sacks back over the opening and closed the door. Nervous sweat soaked his hair and shirt as he descended into the tunnel. The last few rungs were covered with rain water which had seeped into the tunnel during the storm. Breathing heavily, he collapsed into the muddy water.

After catching his breath, he held the lantern up in front of him with one hand and inched along, pushing with his other hand and his knees. The tunnel was only about three feet wide, and the ceiling was so low, only a small child could have stood upright. Eli prayed that his strength would hold out until he reached the end of the tunnel, but already his arms and legs ached from the strain, and his breathing was labored and painful. How far could this tunnel be, he wondered, trying to remember where the woods began behind the house. Sooner than he expected he bumped into another ladder. "Thank God," he panted, as he hoisted himself up the rungs and cautiously pushed open the trap door overhead. Peaking out, he was surprised to find he was in another building, not the woods. Nerva must have missed this, he thought. Judging from the acrid smell that stung his nose, he guessed he was in the abandoned chicken coop which was disappointing, because he thought he had surely crawled farther than that.

Hearing no human sounds, he pushed himself through the opening and banged his head into one of the cages above him. Relieved to be out of the stifling tunnel and above ground, Eli peeped through the narrow windows that lined the walls. In the fading daylight, the farm appeared deserted, not even a distant sound of horses or wagons. It seemed that the medical detachment had not wasted time looking for him and had moved on out for Greeneville. He kept watching as the sky darkened, but still saw no one. He resolved to leave the coop when it was completely dark and run to the woods. Then he could take his time cutting through to the road. If he was lucky, he would be home by dawn.

Clouds scuttled across the moon as Eli left the coop and walked through what was left of the vegetable garden. He felt much stronger walking upright and breathing the sweet, late summer air. In a short time, he reached the dense tree line at the eastern end of the Johnson property and smiled as he stepped into the trees. "We made it Harri," he whispered, reaching for her hand. "We'll be home for breakfast."

———

# *43*

August 25, 1863

Rice sat up all night on the front porch watching for Eli, but he never came. By mid-morning he told Lelia that he was going to ride up the road to look for him. "I'll take Ford with me in case I find him, and he needs help," he said, frowning.

Exhausted from the hard ride the day before, Lelia was still in bed. "Please don't go for too long," she said, yawning. "I'm sure he's all right."

"You rest honey. I'm just gonna ride up the road a bit. I'm not going all the way to the Johnsons'," he said, kissing her gently.

The road had dried out considerably overnight, but it was still slow going for the horses through the rocks and debris. Rice and Ford had just reached the top of the first hill when they saw a circle of horses at the side of the road below. "That look like Mista Patton," Ford said. "What he doin down there?"

Rice shielded his eyes from the sun. "I can't tell from here.

Let's find out."

Picking their way down the gutted road, they reached the circled horses. "Good morning sir," Rice called out. "What's going on?"

John Patton turned and looked up at Rice."It's your father, Rice. We found him here by the road a few minutes ago," he said, but Rice and Ford had already jumped off their horses before he finished speaking. They knelt down beside Eli's lifeless body which was caked with mud and pebbles and blood. Even his beard had turned orange from the red clay giving him an almost clownish appearance. He had a deep gash on the side of his head just above his ear, and his mouth was slightly open as if he was about to speak.

"Looks like he lost his footing and fell coming out of the woods. He must have smashed his head on the rocks," Patton said, pointing to the sliding marks on the steep bank. "I'm very sorry Rice," he added, putting his hand on Rice's shoulder.

Rice shook away Patton's hand. "I never thought Pop had any enemies until you and your friends showed us differently back at the Johnson barn. This doesn't look like an accident to me. I think someone chased him out of the woods, smashed his skull with a rock, and then pushed him down the bank. Or maybe someone found him lying here unconscious from the fall and beat him with one of these rocks to get him out of the way. No, you'll never convince me this was an accident," he said, his voice shaking. Then sighing deeply, he motioned to Ford to help him lift Eli's stiffening body and drape it over his horse. "Let's get you home, Pop."

"We'll follow you," Patton said, as Rice climbed on behind his father's body.

"You can do what you like sir," Rice said, his voice still trembling. "You and your friends brought harm to my parents for no good reason, and now they are gone forever. I can't forget that. I will find revenge if it takes the rest of my life," he added, choking back tears as he rode away.

Patton started to speak, but then stopped and instead motioned to his men to mount their horses. They followed at a distance behind Rice and Ford. When they reached the road that turned off towards his farm, Patton sent one of his men home to get Orpha and bring her to the Marshes'. "Tell her what's happened, and she'll know what's needed," he said simply.

Nerva saw the horses coming and ran to get Lelia. "Somethin's happened," she said in a low voice.

Lelia got out of bed and looked out the window. Squinting into the bright morning sun, she could see Rice and Ford slowly making their way up to the house, and in the distance she recognized her father. She put on her robe and went downstairs with Nerva, just as they rode up. "Oh no, what happened?" she cried out, when she saw Eli's body lying across the horse.

"He didn't make it," Rice whispered, hugging her tightly, and then he sobbed, "They killed him Lelia. He made it all the way through the tunnel and the woods, but then someone beat him to death with a rock."

Morgan walked down from the barn leading Gray. "He already know, Mr. Rice," he said, staring at Eli's body. "He been watchin at the road all mornin. Wouldn't even leave the paddock."

Rice nodded. "I'm not surprised. Gray and Pop have been together for a long time. Horses have a way of knowing when life changes. Let's get some blankets and lay him on the ground, so Gray can see what he already knows."

Everyone stood watching as Gray gently sniffed Eli's body, nuzzling his neck, licking his hands, saying good-bye. Then he whinnied and shook his head, pawed the ground and turned away, walking alone back to the barn.

Nerva and Ford covered Eli with a sheet, and the men carried him to the back porch where his body could be cleaned. Only Lelia, crying softly, stayed behind and turned to her father. "Why are you here Daddy? Did you have something to do with this?"

Patton frowned. "Of course not. How could you think that

Lelia? We were on our way over here to check on you and Rice. We've heard that they're fighting hard toward Knoxville. I just wanted to be sure you were all right. We found Eli's body lying in the ditch by the road. We had just turned him over when Rice and Ford rode up."

"And he was already dead?" she asked.

Patton nodded. "I'm sorry Lelia. There was nothing we could do. I've sent for your mother to help out over here. She'll be here soon."

Lelia looked away. "Thank you Daddy," she said and walked toward the house, unable to bring herself to hug him now.

"Lelia wait," he called. "Rice blames me for what's happened to his father and mother. Maybe now you do too. I suppose there's some truth to it, but I had to do what I believed was best for the Confederacy. If the Union gains full control over Knoxville, things will change around here. East Tennessee will become a Union stronghold again, and I will most likely be persecuted for my beliefs."

Tears slipped down Lelia's cheeks. "I can't talk to you about this now Daddy—maybe never. I never want anything bad to happen to you and Mama, but my life is here with Rice. Now both his parents are gone because of the War, and in some ways because of you. You and I got caught in between and now we're apart," she said softly.

Patton walked towards Lelia with his arms out to hug her, but she turned and ran into the house without looking back. For the first time in years, he felt alone and unsure of himself. He hadn't expected Lelia's resentment, and the idea that he might have lost her forever was overwhelming. He wished Orpha would get there and smooth things over. Then he wouldn't feel like such an outsider.

Inside, Nerva had taken charge of cleaning up Eli's body. She had the men lay him out on fresh sheets on the back porch while she filled wash pans with water, tore up clean rags, and collected towels and soap. Then she shooed everyone away and told Lelia there was coffee and hot water for tea that could be served in the parlor. She cut away Eli's shirt with Harriet's sewing scissors and began cleaning his torso and face. After several shampoos the red clay and pebbles washed out of his beard and hair, and their shiny silver luster was restored. Gently, she wrapped soft rags around his head to cover the oozing gashes. When she looked up, she saw Rice watching her from the doorway. "How'd you know how to do this Nerva?" he asked.

"My Mama used to make me help her. She say takin care of the dead was a livin kindness, a way of helpin them get on to the other side," Nerva said. Wiping the sweat from her brow she handed Rice Eli's cut up shirt. "There be a folded up paper in the pocket."

Rice cradled the shirt on his arm. "Thank you for helping Pop, Nerva. He was happy with your drawing of the tunnel entrance. I know he's grateful for all you're doing here. I've sent Morgan to find Herm and let him know we need a coffin," he said, turning back into the house.

By late afternoon, word of Eli's death had spread throughout Limestone and beyond. Neighbors and friends began stopping with food, and quietly asking questions about how he had died. Each one expressed shock and sadness that anyone would think of harming Eli. Rice and Lelia sat down with the church elders to organize the wake and funeral service, while Orpha managed all the food. John Patton stayed outside greeting neighbors and talking in a low voice. Again and again he emphasized that Eli was already dead when he and his men had found his body by the side of the road. From time to time, the crowd on the lawn was silenced by the din of Confederate troops marching west toward Knoxville. In a strange mix of emotions, some of the crowd smiled and waved in support, while others turned away stone faced. They believed Eli and Harriet would still be with them if the Confederate army and sympathizers hadn't interfered with their lives.

Around six o'clock Rice came out and thanked everyone for coming and announced a wake for Eli the following afternoon at the house and a funeral service on the morning of August 27th at the church. Just as he finished speaking, Herm pulled up with the coffin, and the crowd left hurriedly to give Rice and Lelia some time alone with Eli.

Herm, with Morgan and Ford's help, carried the coffin into the parlor and set it up on sawhorses from the barn, while Orpha and Lelia searched through Eli's closet for his best suit and shirt. Before leaving, Herm looked for Rice and found him sitting alone in the dining room. "He was the best man I knew Rice," he said. "Folks around here will miss him and your mother for the rest of their lives. They just don't know it yet. You wait and see, they'll start coming to you whenever there's trouble, just like they did them."

Rice sighed. "I doubt that Herm. I'm not much like him at all, but thank you for saying so."

"You'll see son," Herm said, laying his hand on Rice's shoulder. "I'll be here tomorrow," he added, as he left for the night.

Rice sat staring out the window. Exhaustion and sadness made his whole body feel too heavy to move. The dread of the next few days was unbearable. He reached into his breast pocket for one of his cigars, thinking that just this one time he'd break the house rule and smoke inside. But then he thought, hell, it was his house now, so why shouldn't he? As he pulled out the cigar, the triangle of paper from Eli's shirt fell on the floor. He had completely forgotten about it until now. As he picked it up, he couldn't help but smile at how small his father had been able to fold the paper. Carefully, he unfolded it and smoothed it out on the table, realizing as he did that it was his father's last diary entry, dated the night before.


*August 24, 1863*

*I'm sitting in the Johnsons' chicken coop. Snuck away from the medical detail before they left for Greeneville late this afternoon. I was told that Colonel Reese Jones had plans for me there. Couldn't imagine they would be good. Rice* and Nerva were right about the tunnel, but once I got down there, I almost died from the poor air and crawling on my hands and knees. It's surely an escape route for a much younger or smaller person I think. When I bumped into another ladder, I took a chance and climbed up for a look. Turned out I was in the chicken coop under some nesting trays. The smell is terrible in here, but I feel better than in the tunnel. I would have never have made it all the way to the woods. The farm is quiet now. I believe all the soldiers are gone. Probably decided not to waste time looking for me. When it's dead dark, I'll run for the woods and then the road.

My eyes have been opened to the desperation of all those poor souls trying to escape North through tunnels, caves and safe houses. It's a hopeless feeling crawling in darkness unable to breath, facing death one way or another. What would they have done without the good families like the Johnsons and Roberts who have risked their own lives—and even given them—to help those begging to get away? Why haven't I been strong enough to help instead of turning a blind eye to the needs of others? Maybe I am truly just a horse trader—not a righteous man at all. When I get home, if Rice and Lelia agree, I will try to mend my ways and offer our farm as a safe house if it's needed.

*Of course, Harri won't like it. She never wanted conflict or risk for us. That hasn't changed. Even though she speaks to me silently now, I can tell when she disapproves by the way she looks at me. It's a great comfort to have her with me, but her spirit is still arguing with me just as she did when she was alive. I have always preached that your faith can help you endure sadness and loss, but in truth it's Harri's spirit and the horses that are keeping me going. It's the same for Rice. He loves Lelia and the horses. Everything else just falls away.*

*I can feel the Devil laughing at me right now. Because if it hadn't been for my obsession for the horses, none of this would have happened. I wouldn't be sitting in a chicken coop, trying to sneak home. Still, I can't wait to get back to them. Dark now, I think I'll just go.*

Rice sat staring at the wrinkled paper. He wondered if he could keep the horse farm and the store going, as if nothing had happened. Would he and Lelia ever be willing to risk everything to help others as his father had suggested, especially now that he was filled with dark ideas of avenging his parents' deaths and punishing Lelia's attackers? He longed for news from Knoxville. If the Union succeeded in gaining full control of the city, it would help bring life back to normal. The supply lines would open, and they might be able to enlarge the barn and eventually reopen the Bee. Maybe Lelia would be able to have children, and they could start a new generation of Marshes and enjoy a good and meaningful life together.

Lelia quietly came in and put her arms around him. "We found a good suit for your father. Mama and Nerva are dressing him now. Except for the bandages on his head, he'll look very handsome for the wake. What's that you're reading?" she asked.

Rice turned and smiled at her. "It's Pop, trying to tell us what to do. Turns out he and Mother are still here with us. Don't be surprised if we see them from time to time," he said, laughing softly.

———

# Acknowledgments

I wish to thank my family and friends who read this novel in various stages and urged me to keep writing and making changes and additions. Their patience and criticisms along the way were invaluable.

I especially want to thank my childhood friend Jana Leach Williams. Many years ago she invited me to spend several summer vacations with her at her grandparents' farm and country store in Limestone, Tennessee. Those adventurous times and happy memories provided the setting for Because Of The Horses.

And, of course, all my love and gratitude to my husband Myles and our daughters Ryan, Annie, and Kate who kept encouraging me for years to, "Just write the book!"

# References

*Afton - A Village of Many Names* (Brochure).

*Andrew Johnson*,
www.history.com/topics/us-presidents/andrew-johnson.

*Battle of Saltville II*, wikipedia.org/wiki/Battle_of_Saltville_II.

Durham, Walter T., State Historian, *The State of State History in Tennessee in 2008 The Underground Railroad in Tennessee to 1865.* Chapter 1 Background and Origins, page 5, Manumission Society. Chapter 7, Landmarks Along the Way, page 80 Kinchen Miller home/Underground Railroad in East Tennessee. (sostngovbuckets.s3.amazonaws.com).

*East Tennessee Bridge-Burning Conspiracy*,
http://en.wikipedia.org/wiki/East_Tennessee_bridge_burning_conspiracy.

*Emancipation Proclamation,*
wikipedia.org/wiki/Emancipation_Proclamation.

Ethier, Eric, *The Big Book of Civil War Sites,*
Rowman & Littlefield, 2011.

Grace, Deborah, *The Horse in the Civil War,*
http://www.reillysbattery.org/Newsletter/Jul00/deborah_grace.htm.

Hagedorn, Ann, *The Untold Story of the Underground Railroad,*
Simon and Schuster, Reprint Edition, February 2004.

Map, *Mountain Region of North Carolina and Tennessee,* Created/
Published U.S. Coast Survey, A.D. Bache, Supt., 1864,Call
Number/Physical Location G3900 1864.N52, Library of Congress
Geography and Map Division, Washington, D.C. 2050-4650 dcu
Control Number 99447157,
https.//www.loc.gov/resource/g3900.cw0053000

Metzger, Paul T., (Brochure) *Jonesboro Presbyterian Church
U.P.U.S.A. Historical Highlights, 1952.*

SparkNotes: Bible: *The Old Testament: Job,*
www.sparknotes.com>...>Literature StudyGuides>Bible:The OldTestament.

Talbott, Tim, *Random Thoughts on History: Civil War Horses and
Mules,*
http://randomthoughtsonhistory.blogspot.com/2009/08/civil-war-
horses-and-mules.html.

Van West, Carroll, (Editor) *Tennessee Encyclopedia of History and
Culture,* http://tennesseeencyclopedia.net

Webb, Jim, *Born Fighting, How The Scotch-Irish Shaped America,*
Broadway Books, Random House, Inc. 2004.